Sylvia Price's book, *Success Is Chasing You*, is worth reading over and over again. She has written, with uncommon candor and transparency, about her struggles and successes as a single parent as she sought to learn how to trust and love God unconditionally. I include this book among my favorites.

—Dr. Earl Allen
President and CEO
Miracle Publications International, Inc.

1/21/07

Jo Dougal

Thank You

Sylvia Price

John 10:10

SUCCESS IS CHASING YOU!

SYLVIA PRICE

SUCCESS IS CHASING YOU by Sylvia Price
Published by Creation House
A Strang Company
600 Rinehart Road
Lake Mary, Florida 32746
www.creationhouse.com

This book or parts thereof may not be reproduced in any form, stored in a retrieval system, or transmitted in any form by any means—electronic, mechanical, photocopy, recording, or otherwise—without prior written permission of the publisher, except as provided by United States of America copyright law.

All Scripture quotations are from the New King James Version of the Bible. Copyright © 1979, 1980, 1982 by Thomas Nelson, Inc., publishers. Used by permission.

Cover design by Terry Clifton

Copyright © 2005 by Sylvia Price
All rights reserved

Library of Congress Control Number: 2005930404
International Standard Book Number: 1-59185-879-8

First Edition

05 06 07 08 09 — 987654321
Printed in the United States of America

This Book of the Law shall not depart from your mouth, but you shall meditate in it day and night, that you may observe to do according to all that is written in it. For then you will make your way prosperous, and then you will have good success.

—Joshua 1:8

The thief does not come except to steal, and to kill, and to destroy. I have come that they may have life, and that they may have it more abundantly.

—John 10:10

I dedicate this book to God, the Author and Finisher of my faith. Going through the process of being molded and shaped into the person He wants me to be was painful and stressful at times, but I stayed focused on Him. I believed, and now know without a doubt, that God does not begin anything without completing it. My hope was in knowing that He would never leave nor forsake me. He has truly been *Jehovah Nissi*, my victory, protection, and banner. When the enemy came in like a flood, God placed a shield of protection around me to keep me from having a nervous breakdown. If it had not been for Him I do not know how I would have made it through it all. God has been *Jehovah Rapha*—my Healer and the Joy of my strength. In my weakness, He made me strong. God is real. He has proven to me that His Word is true.

I also dedicate this book to my deceased mother (Bernice Hampton Jones), and deceased brother (Harold Jones, Jr.). I blow you both a kiss.

Acknowledgments

FIRST OF ALL, I thank God for the Word. Applied with faith, the Word delivers, heals, restores, forgives, and resurrects. It also provides wisdom, discernment, understanding, knowledge, truth, victory, courage, power, purpose, vision, and revelation.

> All Scripture is given by inspiration of God, and is profitable for doctrine, for reproof, for correction, for instruction in righteousness, that the man of God may be complete, thoroughly equipped for every good work.
> —2 TIMOTHY 3:16–17

I thank God for my deceased mother who taught me never to start anything until I know I will finish it. I also thank Him for my children (Andrea and Chris), grandson (Terry, Jr.).

I thank my Pastor, Kirbyjon H. Caldwell, for his love for people, obedience, commitment, and sacrifice. Thank you for breaking through the barriers and going beyond what most people would say, "It doesn't take all of that." Thank you for your boldness and faithfulness by obeying the Word and incorporating the deliverance and miracles and healing ministry to a traditional church. You have made it possible for us to learn the truth. "And you shall know the truth, and the truth shall make you free" (John 8:32).

I thank his wife, Pastor Suzette T. Caldwell, for teaching us to write our prayers using the Lord's Prayer (Matt. 6:9–13) as a model. I also thank her for showing us the six categories of prayers:

1. Praise and worship, thanking God for what He has done

2. Praying God's will, stating only what the Word says

3. Prayer petition, what we expect from God

4. Prayer of forgiveness

5. Prayer for protection

6. Praise and worship, recognizing God for who He is.

He is Sovereign, Ruler, Creator, King of kings, Lord of lords, Eternal God, Everlasting to Everlasting…

I thank the associate pastors Robert Johnson, Velosia Ledet Kibe, and Dr. Earl Allen for their commitment, sacrifice, discipline, obedience, and teaching from their heart. You have set great examples.

I thank Creation House and Strang Communications for my first opportunity. Dreams do come true.

Contents

   Introduction 1

1 *Life Is Wonderful.* 7

2 *Family Matters* 14

3 *Get Your House in Order* 22

4 *Finding Peace and Rest Within* 35

5 *It Is All in the Perspective, Part I* 41

6 *Removing the Thorn* 52

7 *It Is All in the Perspective, Part II* 57

8 *When You Have Done All You Can, Stand* . . 67

9 *Finish the Course* 74

   Conclusion 80

Introduction

> Inform the mind and you change a mind, but touch the heart and you may change a life.
>
> —Steve Siebold

Several times I have been asked, "What do you do when you've done all that you know how to do and you still can't find peace in any of it? How do you get to where you rest in the Lord by trusting Him in every aspect of life, especially during turbulence? How do you get to where your life is based on expecting in unwavering faith to receive the promised blessings of God?"

During my service in ministry, I have discovered that many people suffer from both physical and spiritual illnesses. Their lives are filled with stress due to family turmoil, social matters, and unpleasant work environments. Often these individuals regularly attend church services seeking comfort from the stress of their lives. Unfortunately, they typically leave the same way they arrived—sick, worried, and heavyhearted. Church does not seem to have a long-term impact on their lives, but rather it serves as a bandage merely covering the wound. The bandaged wound may appear healed on the surface, but the root of the problem remains. There are people who have not laughed in years. They are depressed and feel as if they are carrying the weight of the world on their shoulders. Many people just do not seem to know how to be happy, enjoy life, and rejoice in the Lord.

Life has taught me that I should not let stress overwhelm me—and it will not if my life is based on the New Covenant. The New Covenant is a promise to bestow divine grace and blessings on those who obey God and respond to Him in faith. It is for those who accept Jesus Christ as God's Son and commit themselves personally to Him.

The blessings and promises are in the Bible, and when you accept Jesus as your Lord and Savior, as a child of God you are entitled to declare and confess that you are strong, courageous, healed, and living an abundant life filled with all, "glorious riches in Christ Jesus" (Phil. 4:19). God's plan for you contains, "thoughts of peace and not of evil, to give you a future and a hope" (Jer. 29:11).

In these pages you will learn that when you walk in obedience to His Word—by faith and not by sight—you can expect His promises to manifest in your life. *Success is Chasing You* is written in simple format to help you understand that you can achieve success on a daily basis, overcoming all obstacles and challenges by using Godly wisdom, favor, and faith. Using all three makes it possible to achieve anything (in line with God's Word) you can imagine, ask, or think of—including prosperity. (See Ephesians 3:20.)

The *Webster's Dictionary* definition of the term *success* is the attainment of wealth, favor, or eminence (distinction, fame, and importance). I want to add that success is having victory over every situation—I believe a breakthrough over any type of stronghold or bondage is a success.

Introduction

Life's snares do not have to defeat you. You can take them and make them work out for your good. You can use your sicknesses, disappointments, rejections, fears, and uncertainties to move yourself into success and victory. Your strongholds do not have to keep you in bondage, but can be the motivation to help set you free.

I believe I am qualified to write this book because I was a single parent when my son was addicted to drugs, and who is now delivered. God has proven to be Jehovah Gaol—the Redeemer. I am the assistant chief executive officer of a deliverance ministry in a church with over fifteen thousand members. My immediate family had eight deaths in a twelve-month period and a few more over the next three years. I have worked in corporate America for thirty years, twenty-five with my current employer.

It is my prayer that this testimony will empower and inspire you to never lose hope or faith in God. People say that when you tell your testimony, Satan can no longer use it to torment you. Instead of keeping it a secret, I can use my story to help and encourage someone else to go that extra mile. I am sharing my story to demonstrate that you have the ability to take control of your life—with God's help—in the midst of any storm. I offer ways to maintain a balanced and fruitful life—I am a living example that it can be done!

I believe this is a time to refresh and remind people that God's Word will fulfill them wherever they are in life. It is essential that you learn to survive the challenges and overcome the obstacles through faith. I have written this book not only with that goal in mind, but to provide encouragement to believers and entice nonbelievers to consider establishing a relationship with God.

When I left my parent's home and entered the adult world,

SUCCESS is CHASING YOU!

I honestly believed, "Do unto others as you would have them do unto you." I thought life was fair, and that, if I was nice and I worked hard, I would be rewarded with what I deserve. Since then, I have learned that life is a daily battle, the world owes you nothing, nothing in this world is free, and only what you fight for (by working, and walking by faith) do you get.

The difference in my life now is that I am remaining steadfast and grounded in God's Word, mercy, favor, and grace. I am standing firm without falling apart every time I have to deal with uncomfortable or inconvenient interruptions that I would rather ignore. It is important to me to evaluate a person's intentions and apply "tough love" when necessary. Doing so has helped me release the stress of life.

I went through a period in which I thought I had been thrown into a lake of fire. It was a time when I felt like the people I helped while serving in ministry. Since the Word states that Jesus, "is the same yesterday, today, and forever," I decided to try it. (Heb. 13:8). I needed to know that the Word is true, and that it would do what it says it will. I was at the point where it took the kind of faith that enabled me to say, *Okay God, nothing I'm doing is working—if You're real, I need to know now.*

I could do nothing but say, "God, I surrender all." I asked, "What are You trying to teach me, and what am I supposed to learn?" In my heart, I heard Him answer, *Submission—submit to the will of God.* So I did, and confessed, "Thy kingdom come, thy will be done. Amen."

> But seek first the kingdom of God and His righteousness, and all these things shall be added to you.
> —MATTHEW 6:33

Satan tried to abort everything God was repairing but I was determined to get the victory and allow God to perfect everything that was concerning me. I simply had to press through and learn how to wait.

For a while I confided in everyone I knew, seeking consolation. I soon found out that no one is perfect, and we are all pressing toward our high calling and doing the best we can. I realized what I needed was godly wisdom on how to get out of the mess I was in. I soon received the wisdom, but it came at a cost.

I had to adhere to the message of James 4:7, "Therefore submit to God. Resist the devil and he will flee from you." I trusted in everything else—pleasing family, friends, bosses, and co-workers. As a result, I was slowly dying from losing my personality, desires, spirit, hopes, mission, and purpose. Now I had to trust totally in God—and I was not disappointed.

My change has come! *The cost was great,* but I am sill alive. I am stronger, healthier, and wiser. What did not kill me made me stronger. When I heard people say, "I will change nothing for my journey," I did not understand how they could feel that way. Now I can relate. You can let your trials and tribulations move you into prosperity, victory, and, ultimately, success.

Just because my change has come does not mean I won't have problems. Jesus said, "In the world you will have tribulation; but be of good cheer, I have overcome the world" (John 16:33). Now, when life throws me a curve, I know to trust God, and to expect Him to turn things around to my advantage. That is the essence of this book's message.

God had to put me through spiritual school. I will say that I have graduated with a PhD in Life. I have learned the lessons God had for me. I am determined to press on by loving through forgiveness, and when I have done all I can do—just stand, through wisdom. If it was not for my trials and tribulations, I would not have looked deeper inside my spirit for inner strength. I would not have learned to rely on the Holy Spirit. God has equipped you with the Holy Spirit to guide, instruct, correct, support, and help you through life. If you are born again, what you need is already inside of you.

Success is always chasing you, no matter what you are going through. It is when you deal with your problems that you will have your victory—the blessings come after the storm. When I hear people say that they are dealing with something, and they do not want to be bothered, I smile and say, "Don't stress, God is trying to bless you."

CHAPTER 1

Life Is Wonderful

> Because narrow is the gate and difficult is the way which leads to life, and there are few who find it.
> —Matthew 7:14

I HAD TAKEN A DAY off from work, and was sitting at the edge of my garage listening to a local radio station playing the oldies-but-goodies from the seventies. I had been lounging there idly for about thirty minutes, simply reclining in a lawn chair, my arms folded behind my head, legs extended toward the end of the lounger, and feet crossed. Nonchalantly glaring across the way, focused on the beauty of the day while listening to the radio.

A flock of birds was flying back and forth from the neighbor's oak tree to a tree in my backyard. It seemed as if they were racing to see which one would lead, while chirping in harmony, collaborating in song. I thought, *Life is so wonderful. I wouldn't change a thing.*

I had not always felt that quiet and peaceful. I considered myself to be one of the blessed ones as I looked back over my life. I had to pinch myself as a feeling of pride overwhelmed me. Although my path had been difficult, through faith, praying, fasting, and trusting God, I pressed my way through the narrow gate and found the "peace...which surpasses all understanding" (Phil. 4:6–7).

The challenges are still coming one after another. It is like an EKG machine recording a heartbeat quickly oscillating up and down. Instead of pacing itself for a length of time, it would go off again resulting in another emotionally invigorating roller-coaster ride. But I am ecstatic to admit that, finally, I have accepted life and all of the ups and downs that come along with it. They do not affect me anymore. While going through my trials and tribulations, a good friend said, "Just pray; nothing stays the same, and everything changes." During those challenging times, I simply could not accept and casually fit that phrase into my daily walk. I am thankful, however, that I never forgot it.

Each day was filled with such an overloaded to-do list that I could not remember the last time I stopped to appreciate the simple things. But this day, my mind was so relaxed that I reflected on what I considered to be the wonderful times in my life.

Those Were the Days

Eight of us—Sandra, Linda, Brenda, Karen, Robert, Cedric (a.k.a. "Tank"), Michael, and me—grew up together in the same neighborhood and attended the same schools. We were extremely close and did almost everything as an "eight-some." We were like brothers and sisters. Some of us were closer to each other than our own siblings. We were friends for life—or so I thought at the time.

I remember that when Brenda enrolled in a local business school, the rest of us decided it was a good idea and enrolled as well. Robert and Tank pursued drafting diplomas, Michael a welding diploma, and the ladies pursed business diplomas. We all graduated at the same time and began working within the following two weeks, except for Robert who decided to join the military. Michael started working at a welding company, and Tank at an oil company in the drafting department. Tank later returned to school to acquire his bachelor's degree and then pursued his master's degree. Sandra and I began working at an oil and gas company while Karen took a job at a bank. Linda disappeared shortly after graduation.

Sandra decided she needed more money and started working an additional part-time job. Karen and I decided that we generally were not doing anything after work, so a part-time job might not be so bad. The three of us were hired together and worked the same night shift. That only lasted a few weeks, after which we decided to quit.

Michael decided he would take on an additional job cleaning offices at night, but did not like being in the office building alone. Believe it or not, the three of us again were hired to work on the same shift. During the first week, while we were playing around, Michael was showing off trying to demonstrate using the buffer machine. It immediately started spinning out of control. Before it stopped, it knocked a hole in the wall about the size of a large pizza pan. We knew we were in trouble, but we could not stop laughing. It happened so fast we could not have done anything about it. This time we were all fired before we decided to quit.

We started going to the park, sometimes playing cards or simply hanging out. What was really funny was when we ranked on (tease) each other. We all had one rank that would hit home that would cause someone to stop playing.

Things started to change when we noticed Michael was not coming around as much. We found out that he had started using and selling drugs. I missed a couple of Sundays attending church, and had not talked to anyone in our circle. I walked into church one Sunday morning, and there was Michael singing in the choir. The usher directed me to my seat, but I could not keep my eyes on her because I was staring at the choir stand and asking myself, *When did Michael get out of jail? And what's he doing in the choir?*

I guess he felt he always had a place there, since he grew up singing in our church choir. Although Michael had his problems, it did not seem odd that he would come back to where he knew he would be accepted. He did not stay drug free for long, though. I soon heard that he was back to using drugs, had violated his probation, and was sent back to jail. Not long after that, the rest of us started branching off.

As long as I can remember, I always enjoyed attending church and Sunday school. Every now and then, I think about the dinners after church. Everybody brought a dish and desert, and there was always plenty of food.

I remember going to the store to buy my own Bible in junior high school. It was written in simple form and I still have it. I had read it from beginning to end at least three times by the age of twenty-five. A friend told me that there must have been a reason why a person would want to read the Bible from beginning to end. I was just drawn to it. Perhaps God knew the road I was about to take, and He was preparing me by building my foundation and making me stronger. Because that is what it did.

Jesus is the Word and the Word is the Light of the world:

> I have come as a light into the world, that whoever believes in Me should not abide in darkness.
> —John 12:46

Life Is Wonderful

> All Scripture is given by inspiration of God, and is profitable for doctrine, for reproof, for correction, for instruction in righteousness, that the man of God may be complete, thoroughly equipped for every good work.
> —2 Timothy 3:16

The more you hear it, the more your faith is increased. (See Romans 10:17.) The more you read the Word, the more it is implanted in your heart and penetrates your spirit:

> For the word of God is living and powerful, and sharper than any two-edged sword, piercing even to the division of soul and spirit, and of joints and marrow, and is a discerner of the thoughts and intents of the heart.
> —Hebrews 4:12

As you allow the Word into your heart, you will be able to believe and confess it over your life and the lives of others. By confessing and believing it, your life will be redeemed from destruction, and blinders will be removed from your eyes. You will be able to see the Way, the Truth, and the Life that God has given you, "Jesus said to him, 'I am the way, the truth, and the life. No one comes to the Father except through Me'" (John 14:6).

The Word is what helps you to keep a clear and sound mind throughout life. It gives you courage. You are not easily moved or shaken. (See Luke 6:48.) It reminds me of when a hurricane violently blows palm trees and their branches are tossed to and fro, but the trunks never uproot.

When trusting, knowing, and standing on the Word, you become able to persevere through life's ups and downs. Your faith is increased, and you grow from glory to glory. As you receive more of God's glory, the more your light will shine. Your light is what will allow others to see that God is real and working in your life. This will encourage them to think that if God will help you, then He will do the same for them. There is so much evil in this world that people need to see more of God's glory, and that light is in you. Your life can give them hope. (See Matthew 5:16.)

There is one thing certain—no matter who you are or where you are in life, each time you read the Bible it provides answers. Even when I did not completely understand what I was reading, it became evident that God had given me wisdom, truth, knowledge, and revelation. The Bible will help you become wiser and spiritually mature, as well. When you meditate and do what it says, God will honor His Word and make your way prosperous. He will see to it that you, "have good success" (Josh. 1:8).

Separate Ways

Almost every day at lunchtime, I would leave my cold office building and walk around downtown to warm up. On one of the corners, there would be an elderly lady sitting on a stool preaching the gospel and passing out literature. One day while passing by, I heard a familiar voice shouting, "God loves you. Accept His love. Jesus Christ died for your sins. Death without Jesus is hell." She shouted, "Brothers and sisters, God loves you. Repent from your sins. The penalty of sin is death. Faith in Jesus Christ is salvation."

It turned out that the familiar voice was one of the "eightsome," Linda. She was standing next to the elderly lady as if she was her assistant, or was in training to go into the ministry. I had not seen her in awhile, and could not help but wonder if something happened in her life to push her to street ministry? It left me with questions, since she had moved on to this new assignment. Because we were all so close growing up, I assumed that

Life Is Wonderful

she would have shared with her friends if something drastic had happened leading to such a bold shift in her life.

My mother asked me to take her to the grocery store one evening after work. Linda was standing at the door passing out literature and shouting, "Young men and women, don't let the devil have your soul. Repent from your sins, now. God loves you. Accept His love."

The people did not seem too interested; most of them passed by without even looking her way. But she did not seem to care. It was as if she was on a mission for God, and was committed to doing what she believed. Her voice was strong and loud. It was going over the heads of the people in the grocery store parking lot. It seemed she was saying, *you can pay attention to me or not. I have something good for your soul, literature for you to take home, and read when you get ready.* At least she was providing an opportunity to hear and receive the Word. She was already gone when we left the store. That was the last time I saw her.

Never in my wildest dreams would I have imagined my lifelong friends and I would go our separate ways. The wonderful times would not last forever—and my days would not be filled with laugher and fun again for quite some time.

CHAPTER 2

Family Matters

A FEW YEARS HAD PASSED, and it was about the time that real-life, difficult circumstances started coming one behind the other. At the time I thought I was going to lose my mind. I even questioned God as to what was going on in my family. Over a twelve-month period, there were eight deaths in our immediate family, and a few more over the next three years: mother, father, grandmother, grandfather, mother-in-law, father-in-law, youngest brother-in-law, and a cousin.

I visited an elderly cousin seeking guidance. When confiding with her, I asked, "When is the hurting going to stop?" She replied, "Baby, you're going to be all right. When you get as old as I am, nothing is going to bother you. Don't give up. You just keep on living. Take one day at a time, keep standing strong, and you will get stronger." I did not realize it at the time, and I don't think she did either, just how much focus she had given me.

Family Matters

Even today, when things get rough, I think about her saying to me, "Baby, just keep on living, you're going to be okay."

This was the time of the beginning of the family breakdown. Family gatherings were no longer the same. It was as if being together brought back too many sad memories, which negatively impacted everybody. We were all too young to understand what was going on, and no one took charge and insisted that we stick together as a family. Every time we got together, all those bottled up emotions would surface and someone would aggravate someone else until they would leave. We would miss each other so badly when we were apart, but when we got together it was too much to handle.

The younger members of the family started doing what they wanted to do, how they wanted to do it, and when they wanted to. We were all hurting, and unfortunately we began hurting one another by being hateful. Every time we messed up, we blamed it on the family deaths. We became less tolerant of each other. We said sharp, shooting, destructive words to one another and did not care how it was taken. It was as if we felt it was everyone else's problem; we were already hurting so they had to deal with it.

What baffled me is that we began to say we did not have family, and started latching on to others. But that made us feel even worse because we wondered why we could not get alone and stick together. I finally got fed up and questioned them as to how they could have a nice temperament and tolerate other people, but not their family. If they would apply that same amount of work and patience with other people, then they could with each other.

People are the same everywhere you go. Every family has their own drama and issues, and I know the people they were trying hard to please did as well. It should not be so easy to give up on your love ones.

SUCCESS is CHASING YOU!

People sometimes ask, "What's in a name?" Well, the answer is: it's all in the name. Your name is a major part of who you are. Your name is your bloodline, heritage, and history. No matter how much you get on your family members' nerves or dislike each others' ways, you have to work it out and stick together. If not for your generation, then for the next.

Families all over America have been deteriorating for some time now, and it is never too late to turn the wheel around. People will come and go that will make a difference in your life, but your true existence is based on God first, and then family.

I have learned that people really would prefer to hear the truth. The truth helps to alleviate a lot of unnecessary mistakes, pain, and suffering. When a person is not ready to hear the truth, it hurts. But once they get over being offended, they usually began to think that by being truthful, you must genuinely care about them.

One thing God has gifted me with is honesty and truth. I have always been able to be honest and speak the truth simply because, I thought, if God gave me the gift then He intended for me to use it. Most people put on facades and I do not see the point in being that way. You can respect an honest and transparent person on any day. When you talk to them you will hear the truth, and they are not wasting your time. You know they aren't sugarcoating the truth, and for that reason they are trustworthy.

It is important that there is one strong person in the family who is spiritually and morally mature. More than one would be a blessing, but if that is not the case then there should be at least one. This should be someone who will speak the truth in love, with boldness and conviction (whether others want to hear it or not), and assist family members by giving direction. It should be someone who will not exemplify favoritism, but is willing to tackle any issue head-on to bring about respect.

Family Matters

> Then they asked Him, saying, 'Teacher, we know that You say and teach rightly, and You do not show personal favoritism, but teach the way of God in truth.
> —LUKE 20:21

It should be someone who has been through something and has learned wisdom, which will enable them to offer words of encouragement when needed, the way my cousin did when I went to her grieving over my mother's death. It has been over ten years, and that conversation is still just as vivid to me today.

When you ask an elderly person what advice they would leave, regarding family, they usually answer, "Praying, trusting, and having a strong, and solid faith in God." Evidently, putting your trust in the Lord, with all your heart, leaning not on your own understanding, in all ways acknowledging Him, and trusting Him to direct your paths will give you staying power. (See Proverbs 3:4–6.) It has been tried and proven, and if that is what brought them through, it can also bring you through.

It is my opinion that a man is the authority figure of the family, especially when there are boys. If there is not a man to take on the responsibility, a woman, with God's help, will be just as effective. It takes a man to raise a boy into a man. I am sure some single women who have sons would not agree with that statement, but this is a lesson better learned than expressed.

At a younger age, boys are so cute. They love to hug and be with their mothers. But when they reach puberty, other types of needs surface. At that time, mothers should let go and let the father, or another man they trust, take the lead.

There are exceptional mothers who have done remarkably well raising boys, especially when they did not have a choice in raising them alone. However, the ideal is for the man's influence to make a long-lasting, profound effect on a boy, that will help him to grow up into a well-rounded, whole, and complete man.

The father figure that a man represents is just as important to girls as it is to boys. Girls also need to experience, and learn to respect, the authority of a man. When girls grow up with the love of their fathers, they build confidence, self-worth, and self-esteem, especially in relationships. Also, when boys and girls have a good relationship with their father and mother, it helps to eliminate the gender confusion prevalent in homosexuality and lesbianism.

United We Stand

My hometown is Jackson, Mississippi. Most of my family lived in Canton, Misssissippi. My father's name is Isedo Watkins. He was part of the gospel group The Canton Spirituals, along with his father Harvey Watkins, Sr. and brother, Harvey Watkins, Jr. We did not know a lot of extended family members. We were already a small family, and when Mama and grandparents died, that created more division and isolation.

To this day it is still pretty much the same. My aunt told me that as family members got older, they moved away and did not keep in touch. I am happy to say that I still know a few family members, and we are now trying to stay together. It was as if we felt that we had been intentionally abandoned, which led to all types of emotional damage. We are older now, and have come to understand that we had to heal in order to move on. But life has been literally harder not having moral support. I am sure you have heard the old line, "Life is hard, and isn't fair." You can really get the gist of it if your family is not united.

A healthy, united family makes all the difference in the world. Without it, you go out into the world seeking what you are lacking at home. If you feel that you do not fit in the world's "eye view," you at least know you fit in your family's. When your emotions are strengthened by your loved ones, you will not be as needy as many others.

Obedience is Better than Sacrifice

God is love and His love is unconditional toward you. God's love is permanent, it never changes, and it never fails. There is nothing you can do to separate yourself from the love of God. He requires you to:

> Love your enemies, bless those who curse you, do good to those who hate you, and pray for those who spitefully use you and persecute you, that you may be sons of your Father in heaven; for He makes His sun rise on the evil and on the good, and sends rain on the just and on the unjust.
> —Matthew 5:44–45

I know it is hard to comprehend, but obedience is better than sacrifice. When you are obedient to the Word, God will bless your obedience. I have seen it happen over and over. It is your walk, and not the talk, that is going to bring out compassion in other people. Fighting fire with fire only makes them draw back and become more resentful and disobedient. The outcome is—no one wins. When you make the sacrifice to willingly stay calm, have a good attitude, smile, and cooperate, most people will begin to respect your attitude which will change their treatment toward you.

Also, under God's family structure, He considers all believers His children, and your brothers and sisters in Christ as your extended family. In today's society, with divorce and family breakdown, we are experiencing more blended families. Here again, obedience is better than sacrifice.

SUCCESS IS CHASING YOU!

You can have a good relationship with anyone through submitting to God and relying on the Holy Spirit to help you. When you surrender all negative behavior, hostile attitudes, and follow God's leading, you can learn to agree, even when you disagree. It only takes growing to maturity, and making the decision, to do it. I believe it is possible.

Most relationships are hard and require continual attention and work. Your loved ones are special to you. Because of that, you expect to receive love, consideration, and fair treatment. When the unity, harmony, and agreement are broken, you become vulnerable and easily hurt. And when that happens, any slight thing, whether intentional or unintentional, gets blown out of proportion.

Regardless of who the person is, trust and respect must be earned. Once the trust and respect are broken, it is going to require additional work to rebuild and restore them. However, there is no family member who is not worth the effort. No one is perfect. There is going to be something about a person that you are not going to like all of the time. My great-grandmother would say, "Some people require a little bit more work than others. You have to consider the personality of the person, work with them on their level, not how you expect them to be. That's reality."

When everything is going well, Satan is going to try to cause strife, jealousy, chaos, confusion, and division. You can defeat his purpose by resisting him, and staying focused on God until the devil flees from you. (See James 4:7.)

You can love a person, but don't have to like them. With God's help, you can love people the way He loves you. God has given you the power to honor, respect, and cherish others. That is all you are required to do, which means you are capable of spending quality time with one another. Beyond that, you do not owe them anything but to willingly cooperate. Before you can love others, you first must love yourself. You cannot give what you do not have.

It is not a promise of God that life will be easy. You are to treat others just as God treats you. He gives you His loving-kindness and tender mercies every morning. First Corinthians 13 gives an example of God's love.

When you have reached the point of being able to accept people for who they are, when their behavior does not hinder your walk with God, and when you understand that these revelations about God's love are truth, you will have found success.

CHAPTER 3

Get Your House in Order

As God began to promote my work in ministry, I had to get my house in order. Satan would put thoughts in my mind like, *how can you help others when your personal life is a mess?* That is why I am sharing this story— the story of my son's drug use. It is not to humiliate him, but to defeat Satan. Our story is especially for mothers who are facing this challenge with their young adults, and are feeling that parenting is too hard.

If parents give up on their own children, what would make their children think they can ever make it in the world? God gives us children as a blessing, and it is our responsibility to teach, bless, protect, love, and pray for them, even when they are trapped in stubbornness, rebellion, and disobedience. Behind all of those difficult behaviors is still your precious child, who needs your help bringing them back to their God-given senses.

Get Your House in Order

In the midst of all the funerals and grief periods, my son, Chris, unfortunately was falling between the cracks. I was so caught up in my own grief, really missing my mother, that I overlooked that my children were grieving as well. Chris's grades began to drop, and soon he was hanging out with boys I did not know. They started coming around the house, and quite frankly I did not like their appearances, especially when he started copying them. Suddenly, he began to dress like them, wearing his pants way down below his waist, which made me furious. When I was around, he would pull them up. But as soon as I turned my head, he would pull them back down. I realized I was losing control over him, and that really scared me.

I was a college senior, and in my last semester. The only time I had ever missed a class was when the school administration cancelled classes. But one particular day, when I was on my way to class, something kept telling me to go home. I had made it about half a mile from the parking lot when I decided that it was probably best that I follow that nudging.

I made it home, changed clothes, and sat down in my lounge chair. (I thought I might as well relax since I had the evening off.) All at once, thoughts began to press on my mind to go around the corner to look for my son. So I got in my car, and drove around the corner. There he was, walking up the street with a friend. I pointed to him to get in the car, but I noticed that when he attempted to lift his foot, he staggered. I looked at his eyes, and saw that they were red, hazy, and watery, indicating that he was high on some kind of drug. At that point I felt helpless, and overwhelmingly insecure which caused me to totally lose control of my temper. I was furious, and felt I had to do something.

My instincts were out of control, and I drove back around the corner where, by then, several teenagers had started a basketball game in the cul-de-sac. I was so upset that I drove into the middle of the game and stopped right in front of the goal. They all looked at me as if I was crazy. I got out of the car in my housedress, which had holes in the front from being washed over and over, but I did not care. In a rage I asked them, "What did Chris have?" They all looked at me as if I was out of my mind, but I persisted, "What did he have?" No one answered, and I could tell by their facial expressions that they did not appreciate that I had interrupted their basketball game.

I looked up and saw that one of them had the same red, dreary-looking eyes as Chris, so I assumed that they had just gotten high together. I walked up to him and asked him directly, "Tell me, what did Chris have?" A couple of them had an attitude, as if wondering how I had the nerve to talk to them that way. But no one said a word. There was a man bouncing the basketball while looking around the crowd. I was out of control by then, and thought he might jump in and say something. But no one said a word, including the other adult who was there.

After returning home, I realized just how out of control I was. I could have hit one of them by the way I drove up to the basketball goal, because they had to jump out of the way. I went to my room and sat on the side of the bed, asking myself, *What am I going to do about this situation?* I decided that I needed to pray, if for no other reason than to calm my nerves.

So I prayed, *God, I need Your help. Give me the courage and strength to confront Chris every time I notice something, not pretending I don't see anything wrong, and hoping that the problem will go away. Show me just how deep Chris has gone with this, and how serious this problem is. And show me what to do!*

The Lord answered my prayers because it seemed that every time I prayed, when I returned home there were signs of Chris's drug use. I felt that somehow his drug use was my fault, so I

Get Your House in Order

pleaded with the Lord, *Please take this away. Let me wake up and find out that I was dreaming. I don't want to go down this road.*

But sometimes God does not take you out of situations right away. You may have to go through things from time to time, but He promises that He will be with you (see Hebrews 13:5), and will deliver you from them. (See Psalm 34:17.) Your part is to trust Him, His part is to work it all out, and ultimately give you the victory.

No one in their right mind would want to experience that type of emotional stress. But I will honestly say, if it took this time of difficulty for God to bless me with the wisdom, understanding, acceptance, and spiritual maturity I have now, it was worth it. Because of those years of turmoil, I know without a doubt that God is real, He cares, He is timely, He guides, He directs, He instructs, and He will work your madness out. When the enemy comes in like a flood to kill, steal, and destroy, God will raise a standard and be your victory, protection, and banner.

You can sleep soundly at night, knowing that God will fight your battles while you remain at peace. He will warn you and protect you from your enemies. In the midst of all of your troubles, you can have the assurance that "'No weapon formed against you shall prosper, and every tongue which rises against you in judgment you shall condemn. This is the heritage of the servants of the Lord, and their righteousness is from Me,' says the Lord" (Isa. 54:17). What I learned while going through my difficulties is that God knows your potential and destiny. Whatever it takes to get you there, He knows how to break and mold you into that person. Sure enough, I found out there was more to God's instruction to me to get my house in order.

SUCCESS IS CHASING YOU!

Wandering in the Wilderness

Living with a person with an addiction is an experience that I would never wish on anybody. It is totally stressful and emotionally draining. The drugs completely took over Chris's thinking, and there was no reasoning with him. It seemed as if there was no point in even having a discussion with him, because most of the time his answers were lies. Chris lied so much that it became harder and harder to recognize a lie from the truth. He also became clever, crafty, and cunning.

But soon, God gave me the wisdom to discern the difference between a lie and the truth. It reminded me of how employees at a bank are trained to distinguish counterfeit bills from real money. They only use counterfeit dollars in training, and every now and then pass a real dollar through, which made it easier to verify the counterfeit. They learned to feel the difference. It is like refining the ear to only hear what you need to hear in a noisy crowd.

When returning home from work, my routine was to go directly to my room, sit my purse on the dresser, change clothes, and go to the kitchen. After a while, I began to notice that Chris would start a conversation full of laughter, which would make me feel really good because it seemed as though we could still talk. But soon I realized that while he was having those jolly conversations, he was taking money from my purse. He used the conversations to hear where I was so he would know how much time he had to steal from me.

One day, during a conversation, I felt led to walk back to my bedroom. My walk was so quiet that I could not hear my footsteps. When I stopped at my bedroom door, there was Chris taking money from my purse. The most disturbing thing was that he did not show any remorse for getting caught. It was as if

Get Your House in Order

God planned the confrontation because I was just as surprised as he was when we met face-to-face. It is a rude awakening when you find a loved one digging in the secret places of your home to steal from you. The drugs had Chris's mind so bound that he had no guilt about stealing. He could not have cared less that I occasionally got to the gas station or a restaurant, and to my surprise found I did not have money to pay.

Another challenging area was with Chris's anger flashes. There was no normal communication between us. Just asking him a question created chaos. One day, I had just returned home from a stressful day at work and he began to get angry with me. He picked the wrong day, because I had already had all I could take. His eyes were violent, his chest half an inch away from me, and with his fist balled up, he yelled, "I hate you. You make me sick!"

I told him, "If you lay a hand on me, you better kill me, because the police will take you out of here in a body bag." Thank God, the drugs did not control all of his senses, because it worked. He angrily walked away, let out a loud sigh, and punched a hole in the wall. I stood there until the show was over, frozen yet thankful that he did not touch me. We had a few smaller scenes like that afterwards, but never that intense.

What kept me strong in the midst of all of that? I would not accept that a child of mine had any kind of addiction because I knew what the Word says about my seed and my offspring. And I knew that Satan is a liar:

> You are of your father the devil, and the desires of your father you want to do. He was a murderer from the beginning, and does not stand in the truth, because there is no truth in him. When he speaks a lie, he speaks from his own resources, for he is a liar and the father of it.
> —John 8:44

SUCCESS is CHASING YOU!

So I said to Chris, "You're not Chris. You're a person controlling Chris's body." He reacted by really getting angry and screaming, "I am Chris! I am Chris!" When he could not get to my purse, other household items went missing—anything that could be pawned got pawned. Eventually I got to the point where I had had enough. He came through the house upset one day, and when I opened my mouth God poured out the gift of speaking in tongues. It surprised both of us. The syllables kept flying out for about three hours. I had been praying to receive the gift of speaking in tongues.

Speaking in tongues requires complete reliance on God through faith. When you are experiencing the type of darkness I was in, you need God's power. I had to go into Satan's camp and take back what he was trying to steal from me. A male descendant in my bloodline to carry on the family name! Satan is like a thief that comes into your life whose ultimate goal is "to steal, and to kill, and to destroy. I [Jesus] have come that they may have life, and that they may have it more abundantly" (John 10:10). In order to defeat Satan's plans, you will need stronger ammunition, such as the gift of speaking in tongues.

Speaking in tongues is more powerful than Scripture because Satan also knows the Scriptures. He repeated it to Jesus in Luke 4:9–11. Satan cannot decipher speaking in tongues, because it is God's secret code.

While I prayed, God revealed to me what happened that led Chris to start using drugs. God also revealed to me that not only did I have to be strong and not let Chris see me cry, I had to stop complaining about the situation. God let me know that I had to stop blaming myself and feeling guilty about Chris's addiction. One reason is that Chris would use my guilt to make me continue to feel sorry for him. He was not the victim, and I was no longer going to be a victim. I had to take back control of my house. It was a battle, but that was the beginning of getting my house back in order.

It reminds me of the Israelites after God used Moses to lead them out of Egyptian bondage. Because of their murmuring and complaining, God allowed them to wander in the wilderness for forty years. (See Exodus 14.) God had given them instructions for a better life, and had taken care of them all along, performing many miracles on their behalf. But they still complained. So, because of their disobedience, they had to suffer longer. When God revealed all of that to me, I immediately submitted to Him. I had no intentions of staying in that wilderness longer than I had to.

Working It Out for Good

By then, I had started taking Chris to counseling, and one of the counselors said something that really impacted me. She said that when you find out a loved one has cancer or any other life-threatening disease, you immediately take them to the doctor. But for drugs, alcohol, or other addictions, you let pride, shame, guilt, and other excuses stop you for helping them when all of it is sickness. Sickness and addictions are the same, neither is any worse than the other. The process can be tormenting for all involved. I had not thought of it that way.

Yes, it was tormenting for me at times. For instance, when I thought he had tried me in every way he could, Chris came up with something new. Around 1:20 a.m. one Sunday morning, I was awakened by an unfamiliar sound. It was Chris and female laughter coming from his bedroom. At first I told myself that whatever he was doing, I did not want to deal with at that moment. But I kept feeling the nudge in my heart to check it out. So I quietly walked down the hall to his bedroom door and said, "Chris what's going on in there? Open this door right now."

SUCCESS IS CHASING YOU!

He opened the door, standing there in his boxers. I could smell perfume, and the look on his face told the story. A young woman hid behind the door and would not come out. So I said, "I'm going to walk back to my bedroom, and when I turn around I want you out of my house." Sure enough, she ran out of there as fast as she could.

Chris was so upset, he yelled, "I want to go and live with my daddy!" I said, "Well, Chris, looks like we're stuck with each other. You're not expected to like everything about me, and I am not expected to like everything about you. So let's try to get along and make the best of this situation."

One day when I returned home, I found a note he left pinned to the alarm, saying that he had decided to move out. The note said, "We aren't clicking. You're doing your thing, and I need to move out to do mine." I thought to myself, *He doesn't know anything about the streets. I will give him until the end of the month, and I'm sure he'll come back home.*

Almost a month later the phone rang and the caller ID showed the County Jail. When I answered, Chris started talking, "Mama, it's not your fault. You did a good job raising me. This isn't your fault—I'm in jail." I asked, "For what?" He would not say why, and said, "Mama please, don't blame yourself. I made this decision. Don't worry about this, Mama."

Knowing that Chris was in jail caused a hurt that cut deep into my soul. It left me speechless, just moaning and groaning. All I know is that once you have hurt like that, you build up a resistance to pain and nothing will hurt you to that extent again. Your flesh builds a thicker tolerance like a protective wall. From that point on, you are better prepared to handle anything. I have always told my children not to put me in that position. I was used to going to the hospital for different family members who were ill or hurt, but jail is a scary place to me. On top of that, to visit Chris

I had to go alone. I had too much pride to tell anyone why I was going, so it was my secret with God.

While he was in jail, one night around midnight I was awakened and heard in my heart, "What the devil meant for evil God will work it out for your good" (Gen. 50:20, author's paraphrase). Meditating on that scripture kept me from losing my mind. I had done everything I could have done. All I had left to do was trust God, believe His word, and wait on Him:

> Therefore do not worry about tomorrow, for tomorrow will worry about its own things. Sufficient for the day is its own trouble.
> —Matthew 6:34

> Therefore humble yourselves under the mighty hand of God, that He may exalt you in due time, casting all your care upon Him, for He cares for you. Be sober, be vigilant; because your adversary the devil walks about like a roaring lion, seeking whom he may devour. Resist him, steadfast in the faith, knowing that the same sufferings are experienced by your brotherhood in the world.
> —1 Peter 5:6–9

Faithful Friend

I was referred to a Christian lawyer. He said that he was such a good attorney, he did not need to advertise. His name got around by word of mouth. He volunteers at his church as a mentor to help young boys and keep them out of the court system. He told me that he would do his best to help Chris. At that time, my church was on a thirty-day annual fast, which I told the attorney. When he found out the name of Chris's judge, he said, "Chris has a fair judge. I know her well. Keep fasting the entire thirty days for God's favor in this situation."

The church I attend teaches the importance of fasting, and we fast often throughout the year. Fasting has been the vehicle to help me develop an intimate, personal relationship with God, and to hear Him speak to me in my heart. I have been in church all my life, but fasting sped up the process of my spiritual growth from a babe to maturity in my walk with God.

God appointed a fast in (Isaiah 58:6), "Is this not the fast that I have chosen: to loose the bonds of wickedness, to undo the heavy burdens, to let the oppressed go free, and that you break every yoke?" Fasting is abstaining from food for spiritual purposes, and giving God your undivided attention. It is a means to spiritual discipline or to master the fleshly desires in the pursuit of God. When you fast, in whatever manner, the desire for the thing being abstained from should be a reminder of your deeper desire for God, His presence, and favor.

There are several benefits to spiritual fasting: "1) you become more sensitive to the spirit than you can ever be, 2) it helps to redefine your faith, 3) it makes a way for the Holy Spirit to have a free course to operate in your life, 4) is a way to appeal to and interest God, but not change Him, 5) it gain heaven's attention for humanity and mankind, 6) it gives you spiritual power over demon spirits, and 7) it is one of the ways to humble yourself."[1]

God also promises the righteous that His favor would surround them like a shield. (See Psalm 5:12.) This reminds me of the story of Joseph, in which God blessed him with favor. (See Genesis 37–50.) His brothers sold him into slavery, and he was wrongfully accused of rape and thrown into prison. He helped a magician get released from prison who promised he would help him, but was forgotten. No matter how Satan tried to defeat him, he became successful. God took Joseph's persecution and tribulations and used him to bless the nation. While going through trials, my mind stayed focused on that same type of favor God had given Joseph.

At one point, I was so low that I remember praying, *If you are real, I need to know now,* even though I knew He is. God is so merciful that soon after, while sitting in the courtroom during Chris's hearing, a song suddenly came to my mind. It was as if a harmonica was playing the tune in my right ear. It started out faint, and as it got louder, I recognized it as my favorite song, "What A Friend We Have in Jesus." It suddenly dawned on me that God was letting me know He was with me. He said, "I will never leave you nor forsake you" (Heb. 13:5).

After I had gone home, the lawyer called to tell me what happened to Chris, "Chris and two other guys were walking back to their apartment. A policeman smelled marijuana on Chris as he passed him."

Three weeks later, while resting across the bed, the phone rang. This time, the lawyer called me to ask how I was doing, and assured me again not to worry. He cared, and reminded me that he was good at what he does. I am sure he said it to comfort me.

Three days later he called back and said, "The charges have been dismissed and Chris will be released at 2 p.m. tomorrow. You can pick him up after they complete the paperwork."

The following week, Chris and I were out and ran into a girl and two guys who lived in the apartment complex where he had lived. They told us that about two weeks after he was arrested, the police came back and searched the apartment and found drugs. They ended up taking the other two guys he had lived with to jail. Chris and I realized that if he had not been separated from those other two guys, he would have been given serious jail time.

During the time Chris was in jail, I was having thoughts of death. That led me to continue fasting, praying, and trusting God for a turnaround. Remember when I said, "What you fight for you get"? I was not going to give in to Satan's scheme to destroy my child without a fight—the spiritual battle was on.

When Chris returned home, he told me that it was as if his mind was being controlled. He would get so angry about simple things that he would almost black out. He could not get control of his thoughts, and did not know why he couldn't think clearly when making choices. From the stories Chris revealed to me, we believe that if God had not sent his angel (the policemen) to snatch him out of the environment he was in and place him in jail, he could be strung out on drugs or dead right now.

CHAPTER 4

Finding Peace and Rest Within

A FRIEND WAS OVER VISITING me one day when the phone rang. My sister-in-law called to tell me that Robert Jr., my brother, had been rushed to the hospital and that doctors said he probably had a 2 percent chance to live. When she hung up, I just sat there holding the phone in my hand. I told my friend what had happened, but I could not make a decision on what to do next. I was so stunned that I could not even move. So my friend said, "Come on, let's go to the hospital." To this day, I am glad that he was there with me when I got the terrible news. Sure enough, Robert, Jr. died. He would have turned thirty-one-years-old that same week.

Over a period of time, with Christian counseling and faith in God, I had come to accept all of the other family deaths and had made it to the point where it was not hard anymore to talk about them. When Robert, Jr. died, all of those terrible emotions surfaced again. They were the same kind of devastating feelings that I felt after my mother's death. As I had done with her, I began to question why this had to happen to my brother, and at such a young age.

My friend and I made it to the hospital, and, to be honest, I did not want to go through this. He dropped me off at the door and went to park the car in the garage, saying, "Wait for me inside." When we went upstairs, they directed us to a small, cramped waiting room, and we were told that the doctor would be in to talk to us soon. Eventually the doctor did come in, and he told us that Robert Jr. was dying. Apparently, all of his organs had stopped working, except his brain. It seemed as if it was one long, continuous day the following week as the family made the funeral arrangements.

After Robert Jr. died, I had another reality check. One morning, when I stepped out of bed to get ready for work, my legs were weak and I fell to the floor. My neck was like a baby's, bobbling back and forth, and I began to feel ill. I made it to the bathroom just in time. That was when I realized the room seemed to be spinning like a record. I tried to readjust myself to figure out what was going on, but could not. I felt dizzy, and could not even hold my balance.

It was really scary, especially since I was alone. Eventually, I felt good enough to dress myself and then carefully drove to work because my job had a clinic. The nurse was very polite, and offered to get me a soda, took my purse, and led me to a bed.

Now, mind you, we had just buried Robert Jr., and I knew how nice the nurses and doctors could be when they are ready to give you bad news. Her behavior made me paranoid, and I thought, *Oh my God, what's happening. I must have a brain tumor or something worse.*

The doctor wanted to give me an injection that would

immediately put me to sleep, because he wanted me to get plenty of rest. I said, "I have to drive about twenty minutes back home." So he decided to give me a pill instead, but he told me, "If you aren't feeling better in a couple of days, see your family doctor." Sure enough, I did not get better, and I went to see her.

Reality Check

I was usually rushed through my doctor's office, but this time I was given a test similar to a sobriety test. When I failed it, the doctor sat down at her desk and with a big, pretty smile, and politely said that she wanted to talk.

Finally, I said, "Give it to me straight. Do you know what's wrong? Do I have a tumor? Or something worse?"

Basically, she said, "You need rest. Your brain has received a signal that it didn't like, which caused vertigo. It could last from two to six weeks. After that, it could come back at any time. I can give you medication to help you sleep, but there's not a cure for it." She wanted me to go see an ear, nose, and throat doctor if I did not feel any better in a few days, to make sure that I did not have an inner ear infection.

I was not feeling better by then, so I took her advice. After the examination with the ear, nose, and throat doctor, he called me into his office, sat down behind his desk, smiled, and, in a calm voice, said, "Let's talk."

I was instantly frightened again, because I had a flashback to how we were treated at the hospital with Robert's death. That was still fresh on my mind. I very quietly and patiently sat there, and he stared at me for a few minutes. Then he said, "Just as I suspected, you don't have an inner ear infection, but we just wanted to make sure. It's your brain, and there's no other prescription for it but rest—a lot of rest."

I was confused and wondered, *how could this be?* Everything was beginning to fall back into order. I had graduated from college a few months earlier, and Chris was showing signs of consistency in getting off drugs and getting his life together. But the doctor's statement was a reality check. My brain received a signal that it did not like. The news was an emotional overload, and I had not seen it coming. I took my sickness as a warning, and began to concentrate on healing my body, finding peace, and resting within.

Sustaining Fruit

During my illness, God kept leading me to exercise, better nutrition, drinking more water, and proper rest. A coworker gave me a Christian book containing healing scriptures to confess over my body several times a day. I also became very familiar with the Serenity Prayer:

> God grant me the Serenity to accept the things I cannot change, courage to change the things I can, and the wisdom to know the difference.
> —Dr. Reinhold Niebuhr

I was truly focused on pleasing God. I started to seriously consider cleaning out my spirit by submitting everything to Him: my will, mind, emotions, and everything else in my life. The Word says that when you are still, you can know and hear from God. (See Psalm 46:10.) So I stayed quiet and teachable. I fed my spirit daily with the Word. I turned off the radio while driving, and listened to cassette tapes of my favorite sermons. I was building my spirit up so that it would become stronger than my flesh. When the flesh wanted to rise up, my spirit would immediately awaken and the flesh had to relinquish control.

Finding Peace and Rest Within

God was refining me by developing in me the fruit of the Spirit. "But the fruit of the Spirit is love, joy, peace, longsuffering, kindness, goodness, faithfulness, gentleness, self-control. Against such there is no law" (Gal. 5:22–23). You can be going through all kinds of difficult situations, people can be performing all sorts of mayhem around you and plotting evil against you while lying to scandalize your name, but none of that can take away your fruit of the Spirit. The fruit is what is going to sustain you in all your trials, troubles, and tribulations.

I have to admit that I was still scared that something would trigger my head to spin like a top again. So I had to build up enough courage and faith, and believe that I was not going to live my life sick and in fear. I confessed over my body that I would live a complete, long, healthy life. I confessed every day, "I shall not die, but live, and declare the works of the Lord" (Ps. 118:17).

I first heard the term "spinning like a record" from my mother. I can still remember hearing her say, "People will drive you crazy if you let them. They will carry on so much foolishness until it will leave your head spinning like a record." I used to wonder where she got that, and now I know that the saying is true. It is not a myth.

Leap of Faith

I started taking the Bible literally, believing every word, doing what it said, and applying the Word to my life. While I was praying for wisdom, God led me to let some of the people in my life go, and He gave me a prayer on breaking soul ties to help me restore my soul. My prayer was:

> *Father God, in the name of Jesus, I break all unhealthy soul ties that have been attached to my spirit, including the soul*

> *ties from all the deaths of family members and from anybody whom I have allowed my soul to be attached to in an unhealthy way. In Jesus' name I pray. Amen.*

By praying this prayer several times a day, I was taking myself through healing, deliverance, and restoration. For one thing, I had to break the soul ties of the deaths of family members. When my parents and brother died, part of my soul died with them. I also found the courage to let my friend (who drove me to the hospital when my brother died) know that I needed time to regain my strength and get my health back. It was hard ending our relationship because I had become very comfortable with him. But I knew I had to take a leap of faith and believe God would work it all out somehow.

Everything happens for a reason. I believe God had placed that friend in my path at the time I needed him. But I also knew that it was time to move on. I decided to trust that God would bring the right man into my life at the right time. People come into your life for a reason or a season, and for us, that season was up. We made a mutual decision to end our relationship.

The bottom line is, cherish, love, respect, honor, adore, and appreciate you. It is a privilege to be in your right mind. I have seen too many people lately reach age fifty, if they live to reach fifty, and fall apart physically, mentally, and emotionally. Between jobs, spouses, children, and finances, they can no longer cope.

In my opinion, at that age things should start making sense. You have just about done everything, seen everything, and been through everything. If you still have your health and strength, it should be just a matter of being flexible and going through. I was finally starting to learn that for myself by seeing that all of these situations were opportunities to grow—to mature as a person and grow in the Lord.

CHAPTER 5

It Is All in the Perspective, Part I

Success and blessings come when opportunity meets preparation. God is not just going to drop blessings into your lap. God blesses doers of the Word.

> But be doers of the word, and not hearers only, deceiving yourselves.
>
> —James 1:22

> Therefore whoever hears these sayings of Mine, and does them, I will liken him to a wise man who built his house on the rock: and the rain descended, the floods came, and the winds blew and beat on that house; and it did not fall, for it was founded on the rock.
>
> —Matthew 7:24–25

The house that God is speaking of in this passage is symbolic of your temple and your spirit man. One reason God wants you to stay in the Word is so you are not easily shaken and moved when dealing with people. I once heard someone say, "I wouldn't have stress if it wasn't for other people." If you were living on an island alone, life would be easier because everything would be all about you. But that is not practical, and it is best to learn how to deal with the stress of working with people and not letting them stunt your growth or disturb your peace of mind. Getting that understanding will alleviate a lot of stress in your life.

The reality is that you are going to have to pass the flesh test in the company of others. You do not know if you are whole when you spend all your time alone. Whether it is two or a group, more than likely some of these types of emotions will surface: insecurities, low self-esteem, jealousy, envy, controlling, wanting to be the center of attention, stubbornness, pride, arrogance, shyness, feeling left out, competition, selfishness, or ego, which cause tension and stress if your feelings are easily hurt and offended.

It is all in the perspective. Most of the time, the stress that you let others put on you is not even about you. It is how you perceive the situation. Sometimes it takes faith, and requires a lot of work and energy with some people, because they can be difficult and will make your life miserable just by your simply trying to get along with them. They are so hurt, wounded, broken, and hateful that, no matter how much you try to love them, they will not let you. They are in so much emotional bondage that just being in their presence can be draining.

Then there are others who like to play mind games to see how you will react. They know which buttons to push. I call it the "bait of Satan," to disturb your peace and contentment. It can be very tiresome when you are stuck in a relationship that you

It Is All in the Perspective, Part I

cannot get out of, such as with co-workers or in your household. Growing through challenges is painful, but the beauty is that when you grow and learn from it, it can be highly liberating.

God is always with you to help you exemplify character, integrity, and loyalty. Another thing I have learned is to always trust God, not man, and slow down to discern people's intentions in any kind of relationship.

> Beloved, do not believe every spirit, but test the spirits, whether they are of God; because many false prophets have gone out into the world.
> —1 John 4:1

Sometimes, no matter how hard you try, your intelligence, your experiences, and whatever you bring to the table will not matter. People have their own agendas, and nothing you do is going to change that. You have to get stronger, tougher, and get staying power to gain confidence, which comes from experience. It also comes from maintaining a relationship with the Lord.

Replenishing Station

Involvement in church is an important part of a relationship with the Lord. According to my study of the Bible, I have found that the church exists because, as Christ said in Luke 4:18, God has, "anointed Me to preach the gospel to the poor; he has sent Me to heal the brokenhearted, to proclaim liberty to the captives and recovery of sight to the blind, to set at liberty those who are oppressed." It is one of the best ways to hear the good news of the gospel.

As I once heard, it is certain that,

- The Bible will still have the answers.
- Prayer will still work.

SUCCESS IS CHASING YOU!

- The Holy Spirit will still move.
- God will still inhabit the praises of His people.
- There will still be God-anointed preaching.
- There will still be songs of praise.
- God will still pour out blessings upon His people.
- There will still be room at the cross.
- God will still love you.
- God will still save the lost.

When you accept Jesus as your Lord and Savior, you believe in your heart that Jesus died on the cross, that on the third day He rose again, and that you are saved and entitled to the benefits of the New Covenant. Whatever you need is covered under God's promises and blessings. You access them by your obedience to the Word and application of faith.

It is God's will that all should be saved and come into the knowledge of truth. When you know the truth, it will make you free. (See John 8:32.) It is the truth that leads you to walk in the light instead of darkness. Your decisions will be based on truth instead of assumptions. You cannot assume anything—either it is the truth, or it is error.

The following scriptures prove God's desire that all should not die in their sin, but should be saved and receive eternal life:

> The Lord is not slack concerning His promise, as some count slackness, but is longsuffering toward us, not willing that any should perish but that all should come to repentance.
>
> —2 Peter 3:9

> Who desires all men to be saved and to come to the knowledge of the truth.
>
> —1 Timothy 2:4

It Is All in the Perspective, Part I

> He who believes and is baptized will be saved; but he who does not believe will be condemned.
> —Mark 16:16

> For God did not send His Son into the world to condemn the world, but that the world through Him might be saved.
> —John 3:17

> And it shall come to pass that whoever calls on the name of the Lord shall be saved.
> —Acts 2:21

> So they said, "Believe on the Lord Jesus Christ, and you will be saved, you and your household."
> —Acts 16:31

> That if you confess with your mouth the Lord Jesus and believe in your heart that God has raised Him from the dead, you will be saved.
> —Romans 10:9

> For "whoever calls on the name of the Lord shall be saved."
> —Romans 10:13

The benefits of attending church are plentiful. The Holy Spirit will flow and give life to you as a member of the body of Christ. When you attend church with other believers, you are stating that Jesus' (God's only begotten Son) sacrificial death on the cross will remain alive in your heart, and be remembered forever.

Yes, you can watch church on television, but gathering together with other believers provides a unique kind of opportunity to actually feel the presence of God's glory. In His presence is where you are made whole, restored, and healed. The church also provides the opportunity not only to hear preaching and teaching of the Word, but to receive salvation, healing, and deliverance.

There you have the opportunity to fellowship with other believers—praising and worshiping God corporately, which inspires you to not give up. It renews and strengthens your faith.

It is a place that should serve as a replenishing station where you can refuel from the week and receive support and encouragement. You can get encouragement from other means, but God blesses faith. When you step out in faith, it shows God that you seek and believe in His ability to bless your life.

> Ask, and it will be given to you; seek, and you will find; knock, and it will be opened to you.
>
> —Matthew 7:7

God is looking for true worshippers.

> But the hour is coming, and now is, when the true worshipers will worship the Father in spirit and truth; for the Father is seeking such to worship Him.
>
> —John 4:23

> Draw near to God and He will draw near to you.
>
> —James 4:8

> God *is* Spirit, and those who worship Him must worship in spirit and truth.
>
> —John 4:24

> You shall love the Lord your God with all your heart, with all your soul, with all your strength, and with all your mind.
>
> —Luke 10:27

It Is All in the Perspective, Part I

Those who wholeheartedly seek, hunger, and thirst for God will be blessed by attending church. They will not walk out the same way they arrived.

What does the verse mean that says God *is* Spirit, and that those who worship Him must worship in spirit and truth? One meaning is that He wants you to worship Him with humility and passion, totally yielding yourself to Him. Worshiping Him in that manner makes you passionate for His presence and the things of God. Then, no matter what you are doing—whether it is praise and worship, work or play—you will be able to put passion back into it. Passion brings fulfillment, contentment, and builds confidence.

I will never forget the benefits of God, mentioned in His Word:

> Bless the LORD, O my soul; and all that is within me, bless His holy name! Bless the LORD, O my soul, and forget not all His benefits: who forgives all your iniquities, who heals all your diseases, who redeems your life from destruction, who crowns you with lovingkindness and tender mercies, who satisfies your mouth with good things, so that your youth is renewed like the eagle's.
> —PSALM 103:1–5

God is not merely sitting on the throne in heaven, He lives in you when you are born again.

> I will put My Spirit within you and cause you to walk in My statutes, and you will keep My judgments and do them.
> —EZEKIEL 36:27

It does not matter who you are or where you are, when you develop an intimate relationship with God and call His name,

SUCCESS IS CHASING YOU!

He immediately awakens your spirit and starts working in your prayers and in your life.

Make the Best of Life

You often face challenges, beyond dealing with difficult people. For instance, some people enter church, while others enter worldly places seeking, needing, and expecting to have their personal and emotional needs met. But your responsibility is to create your own happiness and laughter.

Everyday is a challenge, but God *is* love. God is the Father, Creator of heaven and earth, and is the only Source that can heal the core of the heart, mind, body, and soul and make you whole. I have heard it said, "Everybody don't have happiness and laughter." But then I remembered I spent a lot of years in misery and despair, and that was time lost that I cannot recapture. That gave me the motivation to live the rest of my life in complete happiness and laughter. From that point on, nothing else mattered. I decided not to take on any more heavy burdens, but to trust God and fight for every promise and blessing He has in store for me. You only live this life once—you might as well make the best of it.

Most people cannot find happiness because they have not met their potential. God gives all of us gifts. After constantly working to improve myself, I kept being overlooked for promotion on my job, which left me frustrated. I finally accepted the fact that if I was going to meet my potential, it was not going to come from my job. I began to pray and ask God to reveal my gifts and talents. God then began to give me ideas and creativity. He opened the doors, and gave me the opportunity to start meeting my potential. God cleared my mind from all the stress, chaos, and confusion of life, and this book is a product of that relief.

It Is All in the Perspective, Part I

You have to learn not to take everything personally, or be over-sensitive and easily offended. We are living in self-righteous, self-centered times. There is a lot of stress in the world: war, terrorism threats, drugs, abortion, hostile work environments, layoffs, uncertainties, HIV, and AIDS. Life is difficult, and at times, overwhelming. When people do not want to be bothered, or they are cranky and difficult, do not take offense and get angry or try to make them act the way you want them to, or to see things your way. Leave them alone and pray for them. You might be the only person praying for their soul.

You never know what is going on behind other peoples' closed doors. Sometimes they are weighed down from dealing with their own stress and problems, and they need some space or to be left alone. They may be using all the inner-strength and faith they can muster. They could just be tired with their daily routines, and do not feel like talking and it is nothing personal. During those times, their only comfort is God's love and grace. It is taking everything they have to press on and pull themselves up, and there is nothing left to give you. So stop getting upset with people when they do not want to be bothered. Stop harboring offenses and playing mind games, "you hurt me, so I'm going to hurt you." Let people off the hook. Once removed from that additional stress in your life, you will be peaceful.

Get a life in order to create balance, so that ill-treatment from others will not be so bothersome. Find a hobby that gives you satisfaction. You have to reinvent a life that is fruitful by being by yourself long enough to learn what you like, dislike, need, and want. We pour out so much of our virtue on others, when what we really need is to spend more time replenishing ourselves.

People like being around others who give off good energy. You should surround yourself with positive, mature, and enthusiastic people to help you stay encouraged. They should be people who can be honest and speak the truth. In other words, someone to hold you accountable and not let you comfortably stay in self-destructive behavior. Every person that has made an impact in my life told me the truth, whether I wanted to hear it or not. The truth stung and I did not like it, but I have not forgotten the impact that person and their comments made on my life. They have moved on, and after I got over my hurt feelings, my life was changed for the better by helping me to grow.

Take Action

You have to stay focused on solutions, positive outcomes, and faith. Whether it is a conversation, relationship, or ministry, my focus is on what I can give, not what I can take away. "There are eight gifts that don't cost you a cent: 1) The gift of listening—but you must really listen, not interrupting, not daydreaming, not being judgmental, or planning your response. Just listening; 2) The gift of affection; 3) The gift of laughter; 4) The gift of a written note or card; 5) The gift of a compliment; 6) The gift of a favor; 7) The gift of solitude—there are times when we want nothing more than to be left alone. Be sensitive to those times and give the gift of solitude to others; and 8) The gift of a cheerful disposition—the easiest way to feel good is to extend a kind word to someone else. Really, it is not that hard to say hello or thank you."[2]

Sickness, accidents, and death happen so quickly. Tomorrow is not promised. Through God's nurturing and ministering, I had the opportunity and privilege to experience sincere love. The world's idea of love can be cold and, sometimes, unsure, conditional, scheduled, shaky, selfish, and draining. God's love gives back, inspires, encourages, revitalizes, is unconditional, is there when you need it, is nurturing, warm, eternal, and fulfilling.

When you have been hurt deeply and overcome it, showing

It Is All in the Perspective, Part I

compassion usually becomes a part of your personality. It really bothers me now when I see someone's mind trapped in bondage—depression, oppression, and possession. God does not want you to be struggling through life with depression, disease, divorce, wayward spouses and children, loneliness, and heavily burdened. Serving as a volunteer at a homeless shelter, hospital, drug/alcohol rehab center, or working in ministry at church are ways to reduce the impact of depression and loneliness. You may not have everything you want, or the money you think you should have, but you will see that there are others worse off than you. You may be the one God uses to say to someone like that, "In the name of Jesus, be healed," and change their life.

These are ways to stay energized:

- Let go and trust God—He will fight your battles. He will give you wisdom to know what to do.

- Resist falling into self-pity—if you are still breathing, there is still hope.

- Strategize a plan and keep trying until you make it work. If one attempt fails, at least you tried it, so move on. Sooner or later, your trying will bring results.

Action is a great restorer and builder of confidence. Inaction is not only the result, but the cause of fear. Perhaps the action you take will be successful. Perhaps a different action or an adjustment will have to follow. But any action is better than no action at all.

—Norman Vincent Peale

CHAPTER 6

Removing the Thorn

AROUND THE TIME I was praying for deliverance from my emotional pain, the associate pastor at my church led a class called "Blessed to be a Blessing." On the second night of the class, the pastor gave an altar call and led us to praise and worship. He instructed us to relinquish everything to God, saying God wanted to bless us. But a lot of us had too much baggage in the way. "Give it all to God," he said, "and don't take it back."

While worshiping, my mind reverted back to the trying and testing times in my life. Just when I thought I could not take anymore, God would give me another level of peace and grace—and He will do the same for you. I could actually feel it. It felt as if anointing oil was being poured on the crown on my head, and running down my face, covering my entire body. God is absolutely loving, powerful, and mighty.

While naming everything on my list, as the pastor had instructed, I felt a snap and heard God's voice in my heart, *I remove the thorn from your side.* God also allowed me to see it actually being removed, and then I felt a warm and nurturing feeling throughout my body. God had begun a divine deliverance of my emotional pain.

I was then able to forgive Chris and everybody else. I still have the memories, but they do not sting like before. All the hurts had been erased. Because of that experience with God, when Chris even looks as if he is slipping, I immediately say, "In the name of Jesus, by the power and authority God has given me, we've been there and done that, and we aren't going there again."

From that point on, things that usually bothered me did not anymore. Where people normally set me off, my flesh didn't rise up. Words just bounced off and no longer penetrated. That was the beginning of my process of dying to the flesh. It is a process because you have to maintain your deliverance. The flesh will always want to take control and be fed with fleshly wants. It takes daily confessing of the Word, discipline, desire, and self-control to not let the flesh have the upper hand again.

I kept confessing, "I forgive you," and listed the names out loud. Soon I noticed that I started feeling lighter, energized, happier, my thinking became clearer, and my memory and mind were sharper. In fact, it became easier for me to be nice to those I forgave because, actually, they contributed to my deliverance. It felt great to be free from being under the power and control of people.

CHANGE YOUR FOCUS

You know you have passed the test of forgiveness when, after all the evil and wickedness you have been through, you can love those who hurt you in spite of it all. Every time I said I forgive,

I still had clear pictures of the memories. But I stayed focused on knowing that I had not gone through all of the persecution, trials, and tribulations for nothing. There will be recompense.

You have to forgive and let people off the hook, even when they are wrong. It is not worth the stress and anxiety that unforgiveness causes. If they are wrong, you have to trust God that He will correct them, or the consequences of their behavior will. When you stay focused on trusting and pleasing God, and not responding to their words or actions, you help them to grow and mature. Otherwise they will move on to someone else to hurt and upset.

As I look back, when I did not let people off the hook and harbored ill feelings toward them, I realize now I was making myself physically and emotionally sick. Eventually, I had high blood pressure, high cholesterol, abnormal thyroid, vertigo, was always tired, had early stages of arthritis, sinusitis, and could not remember a thing. I would be talking to someone and constantly having to stop and say, "I lost my thought."

Not being able to forgive is like cancer eating up the body. I am not a psychiatrist, but I have been around enough people to have learned that most addictions are based on a deep-rooted emotion. Most of the time, it is not being able to forgive the one who hurt or offended them. Whether it was intentional or unintentional, they cannot let it go. They have tried and wanted to let go, but cannot stay focused. I would even go so far as to say that when someone commits murder, rape, domestic violence, or suicide, or has a heart attack, stroke, or something that leads to early death, it could be because they would not forgive others or forgive themselves. The pain and memory cut too deep.

My health is good now. My blood pressure and cholesterol numbers are normal. I feel and look fifteen years younger, and have no traces of arthritis, sinusitis, or vertigo. I did not have to have surgery for the abnormal thyroid. My mind is clearer, my memory is good, feeling weighed down and tired all the time are gone. I am looking forward to enjoying the second half of my life, without focusing on the past, but enjoying the simple things—a smile, laughter, fun, hobbies, volunteering, learning, and meeting interesting people.

I have learned that forgiveness is for you and not the person you do not want to forgive. Now I can say, "Father, forgive them, for they do not know what they do" (Luke 23:34). Success is always chasing you, no matter what you are going through, if you will only look for the positive in all situations.

Choose to Forgive

With God's help, you can forgive and love people by continuing to respect them, being kind, courteous, and compassionate. If I had not gone through the pressures, I would not have prayed harder to tap into the power and strength God has given me. I would not have trusted Him with all my heart and placed my confidence in Him. I would not be hearing God's voice in my heart, giving me wisdom and revelation on how to successfully handle life. I would not have received divine deliverance. Thanks to those who put pressure on me, just because they felt like it, and made my life miserable, I have an intimate and personal relationship with God. God knows my voice and my name. I call on Him and immediately I am in His presence, at the throne of grace.

That was when I realized that deliverance is a beautiful thing. Most people do not want to talk about deliverance. Their first thought is about dealing with Satan, which is true. It is awesome to be set free from the bondage of your mind and healed from deep-rooted oppression. After God delivered me, I was able to love my enemies, bless those who cursed me, do good to those who hated me, and pray for those who spitefully used and persecuted me. (See Matthew 5:44.) When you deal with life and people, and are not consumed by manipulation, intimidation, control, competition, and jealousy, you have freedom.

Laugh at your adversaries and their schemes to keep you down and upset. I soon noticed that every time something caused me stress, it would happen again and again. When Satan figures out what stresses you, he will keep doing that same thing over and over. It is not until something different upsets you that he will then have something new with which to aggravate and torment you.

It takes a conscious decision to not be offended, hurt, angry, bitter, or vengeant. Immediately release your offender by laughing at all their foolishness. Life is too short to be stressed. It takes practice, but you soon will realize that, by laughing at it all, and having the attitude that it's nothing, you will be at ease. Life is bigger than the few people in your life. God has a bigger plan, which is prosperity, success, and victory.

Most people do not want to admit that they need deliverance because of embarrassment and shame. Due to my emotional baggage, I was sabotaging my relationships and causing my own blessings to be placed on hold. That was when I made up my mind to fight a good fight of faith. If I was going to do that, I had to get stronger, tougher, wiser in the Lord, and healthier in my body. Now, I am able to quickly forgive and not harbor offenses. I *choose* to give it all to God. The greatest gift of all is love, and the second one is the gift of forgiveness.

CHAPTER 7

It Is All About Perspective, *Part II*

But those who wait on the LORD shall renew their strength; they shall mount up with wings like eagles, they shall run and not be weary, they shall walk and not faint.

—Isaiah 40:31

WHAT I NEEDED WAS godly wisdom, not people's advice or ideas on what to do. I needed divine revelation, truth, and knowledge for what to do when you have done all that you know how to do, and everything is still out of control and peace does not seem to be coming soon.

One evening, after returning home from work, I sat down on the sofa because I needed to get into the presence of God to relinquish the burdens of the day. Some days are simply harder than others. I put on a praise and worship CD, and began meditating on the Lord. Before I realized it, I was into complete worship. I knew I had pressed into the presence of God when the atmosphere in the room changed and glory filled the room. I felt God's presence so strongly that I could not be comfortable sitting there on the sofa anymore. I needed to bow down and reverence Him. He had proven Himself real to me.

Then I had to stretch out face down on the floor, prostrating myself before the presence of the Lord. I have seen people do that and wondered what they were doing. When you know you are in God's presence, it is like when you insert a plug into a socket, and it receives electricity and power.

For the next few days, as soon as I walked in the door I heard God say in my heart, *Worship Me*. I thought, *My goodness, I must be on to something powerful and special with praise and worship.* From then on, praise and worship has been different for me. No matter where I am, as soon as I say, "Father God, in the name of Jesus," I feel the power of the Holy Spirit awaken in me. It is like a suction that draws the praise and worship up, and I go into a higher level of praise.

Once you have reached that higher level, it is purely worship—divine, loving, holy, precious, refreshing, and revitalizing. You immediately know that you are in another dimension and there is nothing going on but praising and worshipping the God Most High. It is nothing spooky, you are still aware of your surroundings, and you know you are in a safe place. When you are there, you want to stay longer. It is a peaceful place and there is only light, no darkness. For instance, you know there is no drama, no suffering, torment, nothing disgusting, disturbing, discouraging, or disappointing. No cares, concerns, anxiety, or stress, only praising and worshiping God.

While you are there, every shackle, weight, yoke, heavy burden, pain, sickness, and problem is released. Every time I reach that point, tears start flowing from my eyes. You feel totally relaxed, loved, and adored. When you come back to reality, you feel emptied of all heaviness. You feel total confidence in your ability to do anything and everything you can imagine, ask, or think. It feels so great that your body is filled

It Is All in the Perspective, Part II

with energy. You feel a greater level of power and strength, and your faith is definitely increased. It makes you want to run.

That is where you develop a genuine and intimate relationship with God. The more you experience being in that dimension, the more you know you are not alone anymore. You know the Holy Spirit dwells in your heart, and that that is where God will always be. He, "will never leave you nor forsake you" (Heb. 13:5). When you know that God dwells in you, it takes away your neediness and loneliness.

Once you develop a relationship with God, you will know who you are, and whose you are. You will begin to stand up for yourself, love yourself, forgive yourself, know that you are significant, a child of God, precious, fearfully and wonderfully made. Fullness of life, joy, and laughter returns, and no matter what comes your way, nothing will stop you from rejoicing in the Lord with gladness. It restores confidence, self-esteem, self-worth, and the inner-strength that the enduring of life has beaten out of you.

You begin to fight when Satan comes to steal, kill, and destroy, because you know that God is real and Satan can be defeated. You fight against doubt, fear, sickness, chaos, strife, and confusion. It makes it easier to fight against temptation, because you do not want to abuse your body anymore, after being in the atmosphere of pure holiness and love. When you slip and return to the sin that had a grip on you, after awhile your relationship with God begins to turn your tastes away from the sins that tempted you. You will no longer be able to enjoy the sin without conviction. You will know what real love is, and begin to recognize the counterfeit. It gives you a higher outlook on who you are, and on life.

Remember that I said there is no drama in the praise and worship, relationship-with-God dimension? That is because it is holy there, and has a higher degree of love, peace, unity, harmony, and agreement. It is like nothing you can ever imagine.

To get to the throne of grace, you will have to surrender and submit your mind, will, emotions, flesh, and soul to God. I start out by repeating, "my flesh on the decrease, and God be on the increase," until I press past all of my emotions. It is not emotional. There is a difference between being overly emotional, emotionalism, and worship. You totally submit yourself to God, in order to press past your flesh, to reach that dimension. The more you practice, and work on dying to your fleshly desires, the quicker you will get there.

After that experience, you will accept that there must be heaven (God) and hell (Satan), because you will surely be able to distinguish the two once you enter that dimension. It will help you to discern which one you will serve, God or Satan, because once there, you will begin to recognize evil and deception. You will become disgusted with all of that, and realize there is no point in being that way, when you can have total freedom from all forms of darkness. Hallelujah, glory to God.

Since God wanted true worship, I eventually learned to change my language and use the following list of names about who God is. It was not long afterwards that I started trusting and believing that I was on the mark every time I prayed and called His name.

Names of God

- El Elohe—God
- Jehovah Yahweh—I Am Who I Am, I Will Be Who I Will Be
- Jehovah El-Shaddai—God All Sufficient, Lord God Almighty
- Jehovah El Elyon—God Most High
- Jehovah Elohim—All-Powerful God

It Is All in the Perspective, Part II

- Jehovah Adonai—Lord or Master
- Jehovah Jireh—The Lord Will Provide
- Jehovah Rophe—The Lord Who Heals
- Jehovah Gaol—Redeemer (to buy back by paying a price)
- Jehovah Nissi—The Lord is My Banner, Victory, and Protection
- Jehovah M'Kaddesh—The Lord Who Sanctifies (to make whole, set apart for holiness)
- Jehovah Rohi—The Lord Is My Shepherd (I shall not want)
- Jehovah Shalom—The Lord Is Peace
- Jehovah Tsidkenu—The Lord Is Your Righteousness
- Jehovah Sophia—The Wisdom of God
- Jehovah Evaluth—Strength
- Jehovah Palet—Deliverer
- Jehovah Shaphat—Judge
- Jehovah Shammah—The Lord Is There
- Jehovah Abhir—Mighty One
- Jehovah Kadosh—Holy One
- Jehovah El Roi—God Is Seeing; The God Who Opens Your Eyes
- Jehovah Kanna—Jealous
- Jehovah Yesha—Savior
- Jehovah Magen—Shield
- Jehovah Tsaddiq—Righteous One
- Jehovah El-Olam—Everlasting God
- Jehovah El-Berith—God of the Covenant
- Jehovah El-Gibhor—Mighty God
- Jehovah Aur—God, Your Rock
- Jehovah Theotes—Godhead
- Jehovah Logos—The Word of God

Because Satan (hell) is real, you should plead the blood of Jesus often over yourself and your love ones. The blood of

SUCCESS IS CHASING YOU!

Jesus sets the captives free from all yokes of bondage. There is power in the blood of Jesus—it purifies, sanctifies, saves, heals, delivers, washes away all your sins, eases the sin-sick soul, cleanses you from all unrighteousness, and sustains you. From the beginning of the world to its end, there is no place you can look and not see Jesus. He is everywhere and He is everything.

The next time you are feeling despondent over something, don't let it overwhelm you. Immediately begin praising and worshiping. It does not take long before you are refocused, with your peace restored. You will be filled with joy, and you will be able to deal with whatever you become despondent over and move one. It takes some practice and discipline, but the more you do it, the more it becomes more natural and does not seem like extra work.

Speak the Word

When God led me to pray, I heard in my heart, *Worship me and don't ask for a thing.* My prayers were filled with "Please do this, give me that, I need you to..." But now God said to me in my heart, *Speak the Word, stop asking, pleading, and start commanding with expectancy.* The Word tells us, "So shall My word be that goes forth from My mouth; it shall not return to Me void, but it shall accomplish what I please, and it shall prosper in the thing for which I sent it" (Isa. 55:11).

> Now this is the confidence that we have in Him, that if we ask anything according to His will, He hears us. And if we know that He hears us, whatever we ask, we know that we have the petitions that we have asked of Him.
> —1 John 5:14–15

It Is All in the Perspective, Part II

I had to retrain myself to reword my prayers. Eventually I learned, and now when I come against difficult situations and difficult people, I confess scriptures pertaining to the situation. When I need favor, I recite:

> For you, O Lord, will bless the righteous; with favor You will surround him as with a shield.
> —Psalm 5:12

> Let not mercy and truth forsake you; bind them around your neck, write them on the tablet of your heart, and so find favor and high esteem in the sight of God and man.
> —Proverbs 3:3–4

When someone speaks evil, or lies, or gives me a hard time, I quote:

> "No weapon formed against you shall prosper, and every tongue which rises against you in judgment you shall condemn. This is the heritage of the servants of the Lord, and their righteousness is from Me," says the Lord.
> —Isaiah 54:17

When the devil tries to cause me to fear:

> For God has not given us a spirit of fear, but of power and of love and of a sound mind.
> —2 Timothy 1:7

When I can't focus my mind, and my thoughts are rambling:

> For though we walk in the flesh, we do not war according to the flesh. For the weapons of our warfare are not carnal but mighty in God for pulling down strongholds, casting down arguments and every high thing that exalts itself

SUCCESS IS CHASING YOU!

against the knowledge of God, bringing every thought into captivity to the obedience of Christ.

—2 CORINTHIANS 10:3–5

When I am faced with a real challenge:

Behold, I give you the authority to trample on serpents and scorpions, and over all the power of the enemy, and nothing shall by any means hurt you.

—LUKE 10:19

When I need healing:

But He was wounded for our transgressions, he was bruised for our iniquities; the chastisement for our peace was upon Him, and by His stripes we are healed.

—ISAIAH 53:5

My favorite scriptures for handling stress are:

Trust in the LORD with all your heart, and lean not on your own understanding; in all your ways acknowledge Him, and He shall direct your paths.

—PROVERBS 3:5–6

Then your light shall break forth like the morning, your healing shall spring forth speedily, and your righteousness shall go before you; the glory of the LORD shall be your rear guard.

—ISAIAH 58:8

The LORD is my shepherd; I shall not want. He makes me to lie down in green pastures; He leads me beside the still waters. He restores my soul; He leads me in the paths of righteousness for His name's sake. Yea, though I walk

It Is All in the Perspective, Part II

through the valley of the shadow of death, I will fear no evil; for You are with me; Your rod and Your staff, they comfort me. You prepare a table before me in the presence of my enemies; You anoint my head with oil; my cup runs over. Surely goodness and mercy shall follow me all the days of my life; and I will dwell in the house of the LORD forever.

—PSALM 23

The LORD is my light and my salvation; whom shall I fear? The LORD is the strength of my life; of whom shall I be afraid? When the wicked came against me to eat up my flesh, my enemies and foes, they stumbled and fell. Though an army may encamp against me, my heart shall not fear; though war should rise against me, in this I will be confident. One thing I have desired of the LORD, that will I seek: that I may dwell in the house of the LORD all the days of my life, to behold the beauty of the LORD, and to inquire in His temple. For in the time of trouble He shall hide me in His pavilion; in the secret place of His tabernacle He shall hide me; He shall set me high upon a rock. And now my head shall be lifted up above my enemies all around me; therefore I will offer sacrifices of joy in His tabernacle; I will sing, yes, I will sing praises to the LORD. Hear, O LORD, when I cry with my voice! Have mercy also upon me, and answer me. When You said, "Seek My face," my heart said to You, "Your face, LORD, I will seek." Do not hide Your face from me; do not turn Your servant away in anger; You have been my help; do not leave me nor forsake me, O God of my salvation. When my father and my mother forsake me, then the LORD will take care of me. Teach me Your way, O LORD, and lead me in a smooth path, because of my enemies. Do not deliver me to the will of my adversaries; for false witnesses have risen against me, and such as breathe out violence. I would have lost heart, unless I had believed that I would see the goodness of the Lord in the land of the living. Wait on the Lord; be of good courage, and He shall strengthen your heart; wait, I say, on the Lord!

—Psalm 27

When you need perseverance, endurance, tenacity, faith, courage, and wisdom, God is there waiting on you to ask Him for it. These are my favorite scriptures. Add yours to them, and recite them until you are equipped with power, victory, and strength. It is that simple.

CHAPTER 8

When You Have Done All You Can, Stand

Surviving and living your life successfully requires courage. The goals and dreams you are seeking require courage and risk-taking. Learn from the turtle, it only makes progress when it sticks out its neck.

—John Piper

It was hard at times, but I knew that God had given me the inner strength. With His help I could make it. I do not mean tolerating, but dealing with life. During those dreadful days, standing through the hard times developed me into a real, genuine, transparent, trustworthy, peaceful, content, and loving person.

Once I made it to the light, I had to fight for my life to get to this point. And no demon from hell was going to put my mind back into bondage again. I claim that sentiment often, in order to stay encouraged and keep my breakthrough. You should to, no matter what your mountain is. You can speak to it and expect it to move.

For assuredly, I say to you, whoever says to this mountain, 'Be removed and be cast into the sea,' and does not

> doubt in his heart, but believes that those things he says will come to pass, he will have whatever he says.
>
> —Mark 11:23

To succeed you are going to have to decide and declare that no matter what comes your way, you are going to see your destiny. Once people realize you are no longer getting depressed, weary, dreadful, or giving up, it will motivate them to try harder. People need to see strength, to see others succeed, and resist every whim that passes by. They need to see stability in others, because it gives them hope.

People will change when they see you put your faith into action. It is important that God's children get themselves together to be witnesses to others, to show them that it can be done. People do not change until you change. That is why you have to know who you are in God. God's people are more than conquerors.

> Yet in all these things we are more than conquerors through Him who loved us.
>
> —Romans 8:37

God has given you the same strength David displayed against Goliath. The Spirit of the Lord was upon David, and he believed that he could kill the giant with a sling and a rock. And he did. (See 1 Samuel 17:49.) It is the strength of God that is going to push you through, not drugs, alcohol, or abusing others and your body for self-satisfaction. All of that is a temporary fix. Your only sustenance is obedience, trust, and faith in God.

God has proven to be Jehovah Gaol—your Redeemer. My son Chris has been delivered from his drug addiction. He is working and freely gives me money. He tells me that he appreciates me for helping him, and he shows it. I can leave my purse wide open and nothing comes up missing. For a while, I tested him by laying money around, but he did not take it. His light is shining, diminishing all the darkness from his life.

> Behold, the former things have come to pass, and new things I declare; before they spring forth I tell you of them.
> —Isaiah 42:9

The most amazing thing is that my relationship with Chris has been restored. God's time is not our time. God has restored our relationship to before the madness started. He restored the trust, and healed us of all the deep-rooted hurt, shame, and guilt. I still remember how painful it was, but when I think about it all, it makes me even more grateful to God.

God is our Restorer and Redeemer. He can erase all the bad memories and place us in a present where we can go on with life full of joy and laughter, rejoicing in the Lord.

> So I will restore to you the years that the swarming locust has eaten, the crawling locust, the consuming locust, and the chewing locust, my great army which I sent among you.
> —Joel 2:25

When looking at Chris now, and from going through everything we did, I know that when the spirit of the Lord is upon you, you can go astray. But God will do whatever is necessary to develop you into the person He made you to be. Everything happens for a reason. God is omnipotent—all-powerful, omniscient—He knows all things, and omnipresent—He is everywhere.

Having faith in God is what will help you stay focused to the end. You will have to believe, no matter how bleak your circumstances may appear, that God will work it all out. The things we see are temporary. Nothing stays the same, all things passes away.

It is usually when you get that understanding that you do not have to panic, stress, or have anxiety attacks when challenged. That type of faith walk takes a solid and unwavering faith in God as you go through life. The outcome is to go through but not stay in the darkness. Not just see the light, but make it to the light, and then stay in the light.

I would be driving in my car and hear in my heart *faith is*. I would be sitting at work and hear, *faith is,* and realize that the Holy Spirit was speaking to me about faith. So I wrote down what I was hearing Him say in my heart. It truly blessed me, and I believe it will bless you, too.

Faith Is

FAITH...is simple, yet so complicated.

FAITH...is not mere words spoken over a situation that is filled with emotions of merely tolerating, grieving, being anxious, or worrying.

FAITH...permeates the spiritual realm, releasing dreams, visions, hope, purpose, power, destiny, wisdom, knowledge, truth, and revelation.

FAITH...is bringing to the believer that which is unreachable. It is the depths of the soul, beyond your comprehension. It is a mystery.

FAITH...is not what you see, but what you do not see.

FAITH...is a seed. The seed is the Word. The Word is Jesus. The Word of God is alive, powerful, and sharper than any double-edged sword, piercing even to the division of soul and spirit, joints and marrow, and is a discerner of the heart.

FAITH...is confessing the Word daily.

FAITH...is the Word spoken with power, authority, and expectancy.

FAITH...is trust, discipline, obedience, humility, endurance, perseverance, patience, calmness, forgiveness, and submission.

FAITH...is experience and maturity.

FAITH...is the intangible producing the manifestation of God's will.

FAITH...stops you from murmuring and complaining.

FAITH...is common sense, when the world seems cold, dark, and filled with evil and deceit.

FAITH...reminds you that, one day, we will all live in peace.

Have FAITH in your loved ones, and believe they will achieve. Though they do wrong at times,

FAITH...will set them free.

It is by FAITH that I can thank God for my affliction and suffering.

It is through FAITH that I can thank God for my journey.

It is by FAITH that I am not afraid, weary, or tired anymore.

It is by FAITH that life now is easier to bear.

Have FAITH in your situation, even though sometimes it seems we are getting nowhere.

FAITH...is within your reach. Trust it, live it, and walk it—do not just wish for it or talk it.

Free to Live Again

It was time for me to get off this roller-coaster ride. I had learned so much through each situation, and I knew there was more than that to life. I said, "God whatever you want me to learn, I have learned it." I learned it takes faith, trust in God, and leaning not on your own understanding to make it through life's challenges and difficulties. I used to have to understand, figure out, and analyze everything. My interrupting words were, "Yeah, but..." No matter what anyone had to say, I would end it with, "Yeah, but..."

When God delivered me from my over-analyzing, I celebrated the victory. I knew it was a done deal when, one day at work, I was faced with an if I do this or if I do that, what would happen? kind of situation. I heard in my heart, *Obedience. Obey the word. Do what the Word says.*

Sylvia Ann Hampton Price had been reborn, transformed, and made a new creature in Christ.

> Therefore, if anyone is in Christ, he is a new creation; old things have passed away; behold, all things have become new.
> —2 Corinthians 5:17

Like the musician said, "I believe I can fly." So, off I went flying.

My first trip was to Cancun, Mexico. My second trip was to Montego Bay, Jamaica, where I went parasailing. It was great. My third trip was to Las Vegas, which turned out to be my best trip. I went there by myself, too.

I liked the idea of being alone for a change. I did not have to compromise anything. I would eat when and where I wanted, sleep as long I wanted, and go where I wanted, when I was ready with nobody complaining. I did not plan to gamble. I wanted to see mountains, scenery, and the hotel shows. I packed candles, bubble bath, a portable spa, and a CD player with jazz, symphony, and praise and worship CDs to listen to at night while relaxing in the room.

I rented a car to drive up to the mountains, and to cruise around the city. On the way back to the hotel, I drove past a church and decided that Sunday morning I would attend their 9:30 a.m. worship service. On Sunday morning, as the service got underway, the choir stood up to sing, and they all applauded when a gentleman walked up to the microphone. I began to recognize the music. It was the song "Stand." The timing for that song in my life was perfect.

The pastor stood up to preach. He could not start because the congregation was still praising and worshiping. When the pastor finally had a chance to speak, he said, "What do you do when you've done all you can? Just keep on praising and worshiping God. The first place that Satan attacks is the mind. If Satan can prey on, and get inside a man's conscience, he can use him in whatever way he chooses. Satan wants to keep you discouraged, but don't you be discouraged. Trust God. He is able, and you stand." When he said stand, the congregation started shouting again, and the organist started playing the song again.

I looked around and noticed the pastor was dancing in the Spirit, too. People were dancing in the aisles. I guess we all had something we had prayed and cried through. I know I had reasons to dance and shout.

I said, "Hallelujah, I can trust Chris again. Hallelujah, my home is at peace. Hallelujah, my head has not started spinning like a record again. Hallelujah, I had the courage to take this trip, and it has been a blessing. Hallelujah, I am no longer co-dependent on anyone or anything. Hallelujah, I'm free!"

I started thanking God for being there with me during my times of trouble, and for keeping me sane during all the stress. I thanked Him for inspiring me to not give up, and to keep faith after all the deaths and sickness. And I thanked him for giving me His wisdom, direction, and favor.

CHAPTER 9

Finish the Course

You will know your change has come when life in general is not so overwhelming. You have grown to be a person of integrity and character, and your mind remains made up that, though times might get rough, you are going to press on in faith and strength.

> For we walk by faith, not by sight.
> —2 Corinthians 5:7

Walking by faith, and not by sight, is the hardest challenge to face and overcome. Certainly, what is real is real, and is right in your face. You get tired and fed up of going through the same challenges day after day. Sometimes, changes do not come right away. If they do, it seems like it is not soon enough.

So what do you do? You wait on God, who might not change

things when you want Him to, but He is always on time. You stop complaining about how difficult and pitiful your situation is, and put your total confidence in God.

"One basic change in your thinking can mean an end to worry, fear, and control of your future. It is the difference between the winners and losers, the haves and have nots, the weak and the strong. It is seeing oneself as a survivor, and developing rock-solid, bulletproof, I-couldn't-miss-if-I-wanted-to confidence. Confidence to the survivor is what carbon is to steel. Confidence is what separates the good from the great, and the poor from the rich."[3]

Seek, hunger, and thirst for God until you are at the throne of grace. That will be when your prayers get answered, because then you will be in His presence. Relinquish everything—your problems, cares, concerns, burdens, sickness, finances, and people. Tell yourself, *I can't do anything about this, so I'm waiting on God.* Then listen in your heart for His wisdom. In the meantime, ask God to manifest your gifts, talents, passions, destiny, and purpose, then pursue them. That is what's going to rebuild your confidence, self-esteem, self-worth, and self-respect.

God does not mean for you to be idle, so start praising and worshiping Him for the answer as if you already have it. Get into His Word and meditate on it daily. Study scriptures that are specific to your situation. When He reveals the answer to you, accept it without challenging Him.

I make all of this sound easy, but it is not at all. It took me years to get to this point. You never conquer life's challenges completely such that you never have trouble again, but you can endure them and attain the victory in each one much easier with God's guidance. Once you get really tired and fed up, you will change your thinking. You will begin to boldly declare:

> Therefore submit to God. Resist the devil and he will flee from you.
>
> —James 4:7

What have I learned from going through the worst time of my life? There will always be trials and tribulations. When I thought I was going through the "lake of fire," God was actually refining me. In order for God to bless me and take me to the level He wanted me to be, He had to treat me like a tree and shake off all the dead leaves so that I could grow new, fruitful leaves. This was done by healing me from negative emotions, vain imaginations, and strongholds, from the inside out.

> Casting down arguments and every high thing that exalts itself against the knowledge of God, bringing every thought into captivity to the obedience of Christ.
>
> —2 Corinthians 10:5

In order for God to bring on the new, He has to clean out the old.

> Nor do they put new wine into old wineskins, or else the wineskins break, the wine is spilled, and the wineskins are ruined. But they put new wine into new wineskins, and both are preserved.
>
> —Matthew 9:17

Growing in the Process

Living life as a Christian is sometimes hard. When you accept Jesus as your Lord and Savior, you are going to be persecuted. I remember asking myself if I had the courage and strength to continue in this walk. But I realized that I would rather be persecuted for the sake of good (serving God), than persecuted for the sake of evil (serving Satan).

The purpose for suffering is to wean you from the world, so that you can be a witness and set your hope fully in God alone. By enduring suffering you learn patience, and you reach a higher degree of happiness, joy, peace, contentment, and glory in God. In God's glory, you excel in humility, love, tolerance, and compassion for others. You gain confidence and become bold to speak the Gospel without fear.

At the beginning of your Christian walk, God manifests Himself by blessing and speaking to you. You get very excited, and believe that everyone should be just as excited. But sometimes, when you share the Word and your experiences with others, you go through rejection and isolation. Your peace and serenity draw mockery and jealousy.

Christianity is a blessing, but comes at a high cost. The high cost is persecution. Satan does not want you to develop faith and inherit God's wisdom. He knows once you get divine wisdom you can conquer anything. He does not want you to reach your destiny. He is going to fight you in every way he can. It is the pain of suffering that brings stability and hope. Life seems pointless when hope is gone. It is through pain and persecution that you accept God's grace as sufficient, and begin living life with purpose. Suffering causes you to want to get to know God in a real way, to learn His ways, and to obey His Word.

Life is a process and a journey. The ultimate goal of the process is that you come to know God and have a personal relationship with Him. From there, you begin to glorify and praise and worship Him with all your heart, mind, and soul. Going through the process brings you to a point of wanting to get to know your real self. You might have to get rid of behaviors, attitudes, or friends, or even change locations. Sometimes, your surroundings are the problem. It is like crabs in a barrel—no one wants to see anyone else get out or go up. They keep pulling each other back down.

You will want to get rid of everything that is holding you back. You are not satisfied with just living, you desire to seek and find fulfillment. You know that something is missing, so you begin searching for that something. The process is to make you wiser, stronger, and to gain wisdom and courage. It is like being a student. You pass to each successive level until you graduate. If you do not learn the lesson, or conquer the temptation, you stay in the same grade. When you do not grow in the process, you stay stuck in your circumstances and never mature.

During this refining, you are developing your testimony. Your testimony is what takes you through. You learn that you cannot stay in the comfortable nest, but must be pushed out into the world and learn to stand on your own two feet. You have to make career choices, and learn how to balance money. This is the season where the decision and choices you make will affect the rest of your life. You have to learn to trust that the choices and decisions you made were your best at that time. You grow from testimony to testimony, which confirms that there must be a true living God. When you come out of situations, you know that if it had not been for the grace and mercy of God, you would not have sustained your self will and sanity to survive. You begin to trust that God is for you and not against you. You learn that Satan is real and God is real.

Blessings Will Come

The ultimate goal of a journey is to reach your destination. Your journey is where you have survived, and are now ready for the rewards—the fruit of the Spirit. Life is not such a competitive challenge anymore, but is more acceptance and understanding.

You will not be alone if you have God. Do not make the

journey dreadful by becoming bitter, angry, lonely, and frustrated. Push past all the boundaries until you reach the fruit of life. Then you will be able to look back without regrets, and see lessons learned, challenges conquered, and history established for your next generation. An elderly man once said, "I don't regret what I finished, but what I didn't finish."

Did you know that you can make your dreams come true? Do you dream about falling in love, becoming rich, and staying healthy? If you ask for it by faith, you would be surprised by what you could do. Success is surviving all obstacles and challenges through God's wisdom, faith, and favor. Having all three makes it possible to access anything and everything you can imagine, ask, or think—including prosperity. (See Ephesians 3:20.)

Everything you do should be to glorify God. Let go and trust God to fight your battles, then give Him the glory from your deeds and good works. The more you focus on God, the smaller everything else becomes.

I did everything I am telling you about. My change has come! The cost was great, but I am still alive—stronger, healthier, and wiser. My circumstances did not kill me—they made me stronger. The blessings come after the storm.

Conclusion

When I used to hear someone say, "I will change nothing for my journey," I did not understand how they could feel that way. Now I can relate. I have learned that trials and tribulations move you into prosperity, victory, and, ultimately, success. I hope that reading this book has helped you to learn that, too.

Just because my change has come, does not mean I will not have problems. In John 16:33, Jesus said, "In the world you will have tribulation; but be of good cheer, I have overcome the world."

Now, when life throws me a curve, I know to trust God and expect Him to turn things around to my advantage. That is the essence of this book's message.

Success is always chasing you, no matter what you are going through, so stop running from it. Deal with the situation, with

Conclusion

God's help. Grow through difficulties, and process what you learn from them. That is why I have told my story. I hope that it will help and encourage you.

When I hear someone say that they are dealing with something, and they do not want to be bothered, I smile and say, "Don't stress. God is trying to bless you."

When life seems hard and painful, it may be that you are not at the level where God can bless you the way He wants to. God has to stretch, pull, work, and sometimes chastise you until you grow into the necessary potential and capabilities with which He created you. You pray Jabez' prayer, "Oh, that You would bless me indeed, and enlarge my territory" (1 Chron. 4:10), but most people are not where God can bless them.

God does not cause bad things to happen to you. He allows them to happen so He can use them to spur your spiritual maturation, and move you into new levels—from glory to glory. I know He used my situations to put me through spiritual school. I believe I have graduated with a PhD in Life. I have learned the lessons that God had for me, and I am determined to press on by walking in love, in spite of other's lack of forgiveness. When I have done all I can do, I will stand in faith and godly wisdom. If it was not for my trials and tribulations, I would not have looked deeper inside my soul.

It is my desire that this book has encouraged you to do the same. I would not have learned to rely on the Holy Spirit, and neither will you if you look at your situations the wrong way. God has equipped you with the Holy Spirit to guide, instruct, correct, support, and help you through life. If you are born again, what you need is already inside of you.

In these pages, you have seen that laughing at your adversaries and their wicked schemes will keep you from getting upset. I soon began to notice that every time something caused me stress,

SUCCESS IS CHASING YOU!

it would happen again and again. When Satan figures out what stresses you, he will keep doing that same thing repeatedly. It is not until something different upsets you that he will then have something new with which to aggravate you.

It takes a quick decision to not be offended, hurt, angry, bitter, or vengeant. Immediately release your offender by laughing at all of their foolishness. Life is too short to be stressed. It takes practice, but you can do it. You can be at ease by trusting God, laughing at it all, and having the attitude that it's nothing.

Life is bigger than the few difficult people or negative situations in your life. God has a better plan for you—a plan for success!

Conclusion

LIFE IS A GIFT[4]

Life is a challenge... meet it.

Life is a gift... accept it.

Life is an adventure... dare it.

Life is a sorrow... overcome it.

Life is a tragedy... face it.

Life is a duty... perform it.

Life is a game... play it.

Life is a mystery... unfold it.

Life is a song... sing it.

Life is an opportunity... take it.

Life is a journey... complete it.

Life is a promise... fulfill it.

Life is a beauty... praise it.

Life is a struggle... fight it.

Life is a goal... achieve it.

Life is a puzzle... solve it.

One more thing about life. Life is a success... embrace it. God bless you as you press on!

Notes

1. ArchBishop Nicholas Duncan-Williams, (C.A.F.M.) Christian Action Faith Ministries
2. Woody Young, *Christian Book Writers Guide* (Fountain Valley: Joy Publishing, 2001).
3. Norman Vincent Peale, http://www.brainyquote.com/quotes/quotes/n/normanvinc (accessed September 9, 2005).
4. Woody Young, Ibid.

To Contact the Author

Sylvia Price
Words of Wisdom (WOW)
1927 Retriever Lane
Missouri City, TX 77489

E-mail: wisdomsp@aol.com